SECOND CHANCE AT WHISPER CREEK

SOPHIE HAYDON

BAY BOOKS

Second Chance at Whisper Creek
by Sophie Haydon

A woman who values her independence. A playboy who wants to make amends for past mistakes. A trust that has to be earned...

—The Mackenzies—
A Place Called Home
Secrets at Parata Bay
Escape to Shelter Springs
What you See in the Stars
Second Chance at Whisper Creek
Summer at the Lakehouse Café

—Lantern Bay—
Yours to Give
Yours to Treasure
Yours to Cherish
Yours to Keep
Yours Forever
Yours to Love

Find out more at https://sophiehaydon.com

ISBN 978-199-102109-0 (Amazon Print)
ISBN 978-199-102128-1 (Draft2Digital Print)
© 2013 Diana Fraser

CONTENTS

PROLOGUE

"Whisper Creek? On Waiheke Island? James, you must be mad! It makes no financial sense whatsoever to buy into such a small winery."

"I know." James looked away from his laptop screen—where he was skyping Guy, his friend and voice of reason—up to the large TV screen where a mute video was running. A fresh-faced blonde was talking animatedly to the camera. Behind her, rows of grapevines ran down to a glittering azure sea. He looked back at Guy's worried face. "But I want it anyway."

"You're paying over the odds. They've been looking for an investor for months and had no luck. *Yes*, it's good. But it's small, it's basic and it'll need a lot of capital invested to bring it up to scratch. If you want in, at least offer them a lower figure."

"I've already paid the asking price."

"James! Sometimes I think you *really* don't have any regard for money."

James narrowed his eyes. "Such a strange thought." Guy

had no idea that there was very little in this world he had regard for.

Guy shook his head, perplexed. "Is there nothing I can say to make you see sense?"

"No. Sense has nothing to do with this." The camera suddenly zoomed in to the blonde to catch a close up of a smile. James hit the pause button. There were traces of fine lines at the corners of her eyes he didn't remember, and she wore makeup. He smiled to himself. He'd lay a bet that she hadn't wanted to. Small changes. But her hair was the same stunning natural blonde, her eyes the same—bright in color and expression. He was transfixed by those eyes that brought back memories he'd spent the past ten years trying to forget.

"I agree with you there." Guy sighed and leaned back in his chair in an attitude of defeat.

James pressed play again, only turning back to the skype screen once the blonde was replaced by interior shots of a winery. He smiled at Guy, the smile that could get him what he wanted, whenever he wanted it. "But don't worry, Guy. I've not completely lost leave of my senses. I'm checking this investment out personally."

"Well, after you have, why not come and stay a few days with Lucia and me, next week, before you return to the States?"

"Sure." James looked out at the elegant, dark-haired woman waiting patiently for him in his office reception. "Look, I have to go. I'm in the middle of some... delicate negotiations."

"Really? Anything you can share with us?"

"No, not yet. All will be revealed after I return to the States." He glanced briefly at Guy before looking back at the screen. "See you next week then, mate."

Guy's frown turned into a grin. "Before you go, what's the name of the woman?"

James didn't move his eyes from the TV screen. "I didn't say there was a woman involved."

"James." He shook his head in mock despair. "There's *always* some woman involved."

The laptop went blank and James turned back to the TV screen, held up the remote and stopped the video.

Guy was usually right. But not this time. Yes, there was a woman but this wasn't *some* woman. This was *one* woman in particular. A woman he'd lost track of ten years ago after she'd made it quite clear she never wanted to see him again.

But times had changed. *He'd* changed. He needed to see her again. He glanced back at the woman in reception who was flicking through a glossy magazine. He had one week. One week to sort out a mess he'd created all those years ago. One week to find absolution for his past sins. One week before his life changed irrevocably.

Perhaps then he could move on with his life and find the happiness his brothers had found. He doubted it, but just the thought lit a dim light in his bleak soul. He doubted it very much... but he had to try.

CHAPTER ONE

"Susannah! Where are you?"

Susie looked from under the pipe she was fixing, to a pair of roman sandals that hopped impatiently from side to side. "Under here! What is it?" She continued to tighten the bolt with the spanner.

"Pete's here and he's got someone with him. He wants you."

"Pete?" Susie frowned but continued to work the spanner. "He's meant to be on his way to Christchurch."

"He *will* be later on today. But he's here now, and he wants to see you." The sandals were joined by a concerned-looking face framed with corkscrew curls, as Jorja, the winery receptionist, knelt down and peered at Susie. "It looks serious. Pete's all dressed up in a suit and so is this other guy." She gave a long, low whistle of approval.

Susie closed her eyes and sighed. A suit, a stranger? Pete never wore suits and certainly no one ever came to the winery in suits. Shorts, jandals, backpacks, yes, but suits? No way. It could only mean one thing. Pete had sold the winery. He'd been looking for a buyer for months. It must have happened while he was in the South Island, because she had *no* clue anyone was interested. Susie gave the bolt a final, unnecessary, twist.

"Okay, I'm coming."

She wriggled out from under the pipe work and brushed herself down, managing to smear oil down her shorts as she did so. Jorja eyed her up and down nervously. "You'd better get changed. This looks serious."

"No way. This is a working winery. Whoever this guy is will have to take me as I am."

"They're in the boardroom," Jorja whispered, opening the door.

Susie followed Jorja out to the small reception area, where she heard the low murmur of male voices. "Board-room? Since when have we had a boardroom?"

"Since Pete wanted to impress someone. I even had to photocopy papers for you. They looked *really* official."

Susie's heart sank. Her first guess must have been correct. "I suppose it had to happen."

Jorja smiled sympathetically. "It'll probably carry on as before. Why else would anyone buy the winery? They must have fallen in love with it like we have."

"Let's hope so." She walked into the high-ceilinged room, more often used for wine tasting than meetings, and looked around. Pete was standing, alone, beside the open ranch sliders.

"Susannah!" He grinned and walked quickly over and planted a friendly kiss on the side of her cheek. And, for the umpteenth time, Susie wondered why she couldn't feel anything more than friendship for this wonderful man.

"Hey, you! I thought you were on your way to Christchurch?"

"I'm still going. I'm leaving in an hour. It's just a flying visit. For me, at least."

Susie frowned. "What do you mean?"

"You'll never believe it." His mouth twisted as he tried, in vain, to suppress a grin.

"You've sold up?" She said mournfully, helping herself to a handful of raw nuts that Jorja had tipped into a wooden bowl.

"Yep! Out of blue."

"How come you didn't tell me?"

"I tried to contact you."

"Ah... I was camping, with Tom. I didn't take my cell phone."

"Anyway, I knew you'd be happy. It's what we've both been wanting—an investor who doesn't want to close us down or amalgamate with another winery. It's perfect."

"Okay, slow down. How did it happen?"

"I was down in Shelter Springs—"

She raised an eyebrow. "With the lovely Lizzi at The Lakehouse Café, so I hear."

"How did you know?"

"It's a small place."

He shrugged. "Anyway, it was through her that I found him."

Susie looked up suddenly. "Found who?"

Pete thrust his hands in his pockets and rolled back onto his heels, a self-satisfied smile on his face. "The new owner of Whisper Creek winery."

Suddenly Susie became aware of voices on the terrace. Jorja had moved outside and her soft lilting Scots accent drifted in through the open window. But now another voice had joined hers—deep, masculine, and as seductive and warming as the soft afternoon breeze. Her mouth went dry as a sickening jolt of visceral recognition gripped her. She *knew* that voice. She might not have heard it in ten years, but it was as familiar to her as her own. But her mind refused to believe what her body was telling her. She turned slowly to Pete, who was uncorking a bottle of wine, and tried to speak but no sound emerged. She swallowed. "Who is it?"

The disembodied voice stopped at what sounded like the punch line to a joke and Jorja's flirtatious laughter followed. Susie shook her head, as if to rid it of an unwelcome echo. But, even though she could no longer hear it, the voice filled her senses.

Pete pulled the cork out with a pop and turned to her. "Who is what?"

"The new owner, Pete. *Who* is the new owner?"

"JM Investments." He sniffed the wine appreciatively. "It's a holding company which owns several wineries including one in Napa Valley."

He poured the wine into three burgundy glasses and she inhaled a deep breath as she automatically took the glass Pete offered her. "And it's owned by?"

The afternoon sun suddenly shadowed as someone stood in the doorway.

"James—" Pete began.

"Mackenzie," the voice interrupted. She looked up at the man whose shadow reached over the clay-tiled floor and touched her. His dark silhouette was outlined by the late sun and she couldn't see his features clearly. But she would have known his voice anywhere, known the man, from how his gaze made her feel.

Then he stepped towards her into the light. She knew the lines of his face like she knew her own. It was at once familiar and yet also strange. The familiar lines—the shape of his face, his nose, cheekbones— had morphed from a fun-loving, good-looking teen into an unfamiliar figure—an immaculately dressed, devastatingly handsome man. But the humor in his eyes was still there and the smile on his lips was the same as he extended his hand towards hers.

Pete cleared his throat and shifted his feet. "Susannah?" He laughed uncomfortably. "James, this is Susannah Henderson, who's not normally at a loss for words."

"It seems I've made her speechless." Her heart beat loudly in her ears as he reached further for her hand and shook it. "Hello, *Susannah*." He stressed her name, giving it a faint question mark. Of course, he'd never called her by that name before.

She tried to contain the jolt of recognition as his hand gripped hers in a handshake that he seemed in no hurry to break. She looked down, embarrassed by the flare of heat she knew had flooded her pale skin.

Susie opened her mouth to speak but nothing came out at first. She gulped in a deep breath. "James... Mackenzie."

He smiled. "Correct. But the names are usually run on together, without the long pause in the middle."

"I *know* how the name is pronounced."

She looked down at their hands, which were still joined in a handshake. James slowly relaxed his grip and she let her hand fall and turned away.

Pete hadn't seemed to notice the awkward moment as he passed James a glass of wine. "Susannah's my right-hand woman. Runs the place really. She does everything, even helping the wine-maker who we share with a couple of other local wineries. Been with me the past eight years, haven't you?" He pulled her to him and gave her a brotherly hug. "What Susannah doesn't know about the place, isn't worth knowing."

"Then we'll have a lot to discuss over the next week."

Her blood pressure skyrocketed as she felt the full blast of James's gaze and words. She swallowed a gasp and turned away.

"A week?" Her voice emerged as a husky whisper that Pete didn't hear.

Pete held up the wine to the light. "This is the top of our line. You tasted last year's vintage in the South Island. This one"—he held up the ruby red wine, now enflamed by the late sun—"is five years old and sells at our premium price."

James reached over and tapped his glass against hers and then Pete's. "Here's to your future, Pete. All the best."

She tried to speak but couldn't. Beads of sweat prickled her brow.

"The future!" Pete grinned and turned to Susie. "Are you okay?"

"Just hot." She placed the glass on the table and pushed open a window, taking in a gulp of the warm salty air. She half-listened to Pete talking about the wine, about the island, about the future of the winery. Her future. Alone. Or it had been up until now. His words flowed and settled around her like oil on water, covering her confusion but not resolving it.

She took a deep breath and slowly turned back around. Pete was holding up the glass of wine to the light and describing its qualities, but James? James remained standing where he'd stood before, his eyes still on her. Except the smile was no longer there, it was replaced by a look she didn't recognize and couldn't read. Their wordless gaze was interrupted by the entrance of other winery staff.

"James, let me introduce you to the rest of our team."

Pete glanced at his watch. "We've got just under an hour before I leave. Sorry to rush away."

"No problem. With so little notice, I appreciate you coming here at all."

Susie sat down at the opposite end of the table and glanced through the business papers Pete had distributed, barely aware of the ebb and flow of conversation. She was aware only of James's physical presence and the whirling mix of contradictory emotions—confusion, excitement, fear and something else she refused to contemplate. No, she wasn't going there. There was only one thing she needed to know—what the hell he was doing here, after all these years. Because of him, her and her family's lives had been destroyed ten years before. She'd made a new life for herself through sheer hard work but her father had died a broken man, his livelihood and dreams, shattered. Had James bought the winery to rob her of her dreams once more? To take her hard-earned position with the company away from her?

She watched as he leaned back in his chair—totally at ease, as he charmed both men and women alike—and his hand absent-mindedly smoothed the highly polished desk, as if reveling in its silky texture. A forgotten memory of how he'd enjoyed working with wood as a young boy, flashed into her mind. It had been a part of him then, something real but, no doubt, long forgotten—the only remnant being his sensual response to the wood. She doubted he was even aware of the sensuality of his action. Everything had always been instinctive with James. Including seducing her.

"Don't we, Susannah?"

Startled, Susie turned quickly to Pete. He'd been speaking and she'd missed the question entirely.

"Sorry, what were you saying?"

Pete gave an uncomfortable laugh. "I was just saying how well we work as a team." He glanced at James. "Susannah's usually extremely focused, able to give you facts and figures off the top of her head. The winery wouldn't be what it is without her."

"So I hear." James's seductive voice snaked its way around and through her body, stimulating her senses like the soft trail of a finger along delicate skin. His softened tone forced her to look up. He was still looking directly at her, just as he had when he'd entered the room.

She couldn't let him get to her. She had to play it cool. His money might be Pete's ticket off Waiheke, but she needed to find out what he wanted before his money destroyed her. She cleared her throat. "Pete and I have worked as a team up till now, with the help of a local winemaker. But I'm more than happy, *capable*, of running the business on my own. Could you tell me, Mr. Mackenzie—"

"James, please—"

"Mr. Mackenzie," she repeated firmly. "What it is you expect in return for your investment?"

There was a deafening, surprised, silence. James leaned forward across the desk, his hand loosely clasped before him, his shoulders relaxed, his eyes amused, a slight smile playing on his lips. "What do I expect? Are you concerned that I expect too much?"

"Frankly, yes."

He'd understood what she'd meant. She could see it in his narrowed, knowing gaze. He sat back in his chair, the smile now gone. "I expect a well-run business. I expect a return on my investment. I *expect*, Mrs Henderson, it is Mrs, isn't it?"

She nodded.

"I *expect* to work closely with the management team to achieve these things."

"Um." Susie pressed her lips together in disapproval. "Interesting list. It could be applied to a manufacturer of just about anything."

A fidgety hand was placed on her arm. She glanced at Pete's frowning face. "Susannah." His tone held a warning.

She turned back to James. "We make *wines*."

"*That* hadn't escaped my notice. But thank you for the reminder."

"We're a boutique winery, we're individual, we're not a mass market winery that will add significantly to your bottom line."

Pete's grip on her arm tightened. "Susannah!" The warning was stronger this time.

"Pete, it's fine," James reassured. "It's best to be clear about my intentions from the beginning. That way no one is under any illusions." James looked at Susie once more. "I have extensive wine holdings and an investment in a small up-and-coming vineyard fits into our plans."

"Why? What are your plans?"

"That, Mrs Henderson, I believe is *my* business." James's voice was quiet but firm. The humor had dropped from his eyes and they now held only challenge. "Suffice to say, I'm very aware of what Whisper Creek has to offer and have no intention of changing its strengths and brand."

Susie sat back in the hard, oak-backed chair, only partially reassured.

"But," James continued, "I have every intention of building on them and making it the profitable company I believe it could be."

"Perfect!" Pete jumped up, obviously anxious to avoid any further tension. "So, if everyone's happy?" Pete gave

Susie a warning glance. "Let's move on to the serious business of eating and drinking. Time's slipping by and I'll need to leave soon to catch the ferry."

She nodded hesitantly. The buy-out was a fantastic windfall for Pete and it *should* be a fantastic opportunity for her. It would ensure the future of the winery. It would ensure *her* future. But it was *Mac*. Her nickname for him popped up into her mind, driven deep through years of heartache. But it had survived. What else had survived of their relationship? Was it really business, or was there something personal behind the investment? She didn't trust him. She had no *reason* to trust him.

She gave the pen a twirl on the desk, before suddenly grabbing it. She clasped it in her hand and brought it up in front of her face, clenching it lightly. She grimaced. "I'm sorry, something's bothering me, something's not quite right here."

She heard Pete groan but she couldn't go back now.

She looked directly at Mac. This was between him and her. It had nothing to do with Pete. "Something's...not right...Mr. Mackenzie," she repeated softly.

He remained motionless, his white shirt, open-necked under his exquisitely cut silk suit. Tanned, blue, blue eyes and dark hair. How could anyone be so handsome? How could a man be so handsome, when she was so plain? How could she have allowed herself to feel—to *have* felt, she reminded herself—so much for someone who had always been so patently out of her league?

His eyes were intense as they stared back at her, his brows knitted together in a slight frown as if trying to understand something. "Is that so? And what can I do to persuade you that everything is absolutely right, that everything *is* just as it should be?"

She focused on her breathing as she tried to control her instinctive reaction to him. She cleared her throat and tried to pull her eyes away from Mac's face, but they only shifted down to his hands, loosely steepled on the table, as if the tension between them didn't exist. Or perhaps, unlike her, he felt it but was capable of dealing with it.

"Susannah." Pete's voice was strained as he tried not to overrule her in public. She held up her hand to him.

"It's my future, Pete, I need to know what's going on." Her eyes flicked up to Mac's eyes once more. "How can you persuade me that everything's as it should be? By being honest with what you want from this arrangement. We're a small company, insignificant by your standards. What can we possibly offer you?"

She could see in his eyes that he knew what she was really asking.

"An opportunity to get back to basics. To start afresh. One doesn't often get given that opportunity—to create something new. Is that honest enough for you, Susie?"

The name by which he'd always called her, slipped out and surprised everyone, breaking the spell, confounding and deepening the atmosphere.

Pete looked from one to the other. "So... do you two... know each other?"

"Yes. Coincidence, isn't it?" Susie addressed her remark to James, not Pete.

"Coincidence?" James paused. "No, not really."

"Care to elaborate?" Susie heard the chill in her voice.

James turned to Pete. "My sister-in-law, Gemma, passed on your brochure and DVD which Lizzi, at the Lakehouse Café, had given her." He turned back to Susie. "I watched the video and I saw... a familiar face. Not"—he inclined his head to Susie—"a familiar name." He turned to

Pete. "I knew Susie as Susie Shaw, not Susannah Henderson."

"Henderson is my married name."

"Anyway." He shrugged. "One look at the video and I was hooked."

Susie ground her teeth. Damn that video. She knew she should never have done it. It wasn't her thing, but Pete had persuaded her because no one knew the winery better than she did.

Pete nodded. "Ah, well, that explains it. So, shall we have a quick tour of the winery before we leave?"

"Perfect." James's gaze returned to Susie, having barely glanced at Pete.

Pete opened the door and James rose with his usual graceful ease and walked out into the lobby with Pete. He'd always been aware of his body, and how to use it. Instinctively she brushed down her work shorts, conscious of the difference in their appearance. It made her feel at a disadvantage and she made a mental note that this would be the last time she felt like that.

She glanced around and saw James had left some papers on the table. Just at that moment he returned, by himself.

She picked up the papers and held them out to him. "Grown forgetful?"

He shook his head, no sign of a smile now. "No. I remember everything."

"And you *still* choose to come here and buy a company I'm involved with? I'm surprised."

"Are you? Why?" Again, he was being deliberately obtuse.

"Oh, I don't know," she said, layering the sarcasm thickly. "Perhaps because ten years ago I told you I never wanted to see you again?" She could see she'd hit a raw nerve by the tension in the fine lines around his eyes that she hadn't noticed before. His face was immobile and, for the first time, serious.

"Ten years is a long time."

"Not so long when the facts remain the same, when the feelings remain the same. When nothing's changed."

"And that's where you're wrong."

"No, I'm not. You were a bastard then, and I'm sure you're a bastard now."

He shrugged. "A bastard maybe, but I'm also the owner of this winery." He tapped the papers he was still holding, onto the table between them. "Signed and sealed. *Everything* has changed."

She felt as if she'd been struck, winded. She sucked in a deep breath, desperately trying to regain her sense of self-possession. She *never* lost it. She was *always* in control, *always* in charge, since James had left, anyway.

"Everything? You want to change the winery?"

"That depends on what I find."

Susie looked at James, acutely aware of the warning in his answer. "And what is it you're looking for?" The shadow of sorrow she'd seen in his eyes earlier, deepened, casting a corresponding shadow on her own soul, like it or not.

"What I'm always looking for, Susie."

"Entertainment? Bored are we?"

He was standing too close to her now and she smelt his aftershave, subtle and potent. "I'm after satisfaction." His breath was warm against her skin, which prickled with awareness. She struggled to keep her breathing even.

"Satisfaction for a spoiled, bored womanizer with more money than he knows what to do with?"

She was irritated to note that, rather than being

offended, a smile tugged at his lips. "You *have* been following me then. I'm flattered."

"Don't be. It's hard not to come across someone whose every move is recorded faithfully in the tabloids." She shrugged deliberately but it was too stiff to be convincing. "You've *been* everywhere, *with* everyone and you're bored. But you won't find satisfaction here. You'll need all the time in the world to get that. You won't get it from investing funds in a small winery. You won't get it from one week on Waiheke Island."

"Really? Then perhaps I should stay longer."

Susie's heart sank. "No way." She shook her head.

"No need to panic. I'm kidding. One week is all I have left."

"All you have *left*? I'd have thought someone with your money would be free to do whatever you liked."

"Not after next week."

She frowned, but before she could respond, Pete walked quickly into the room. "Time's slipping by, James. Would you like a quick tour before you go?"

"Sure." He turned abruptly to Pete and smiled. "And then perhaps dinner tonight with Susie and a longer tour tomorrow."

"Great idea." Pete looked from one to the other. "If that's okay with you, Susannah? It won't interfere with any arrangements with Tom, will it?"

Susie shook her head, wishing Tom hadn't been mentioned. The tension that had gripped her from the moment she'd heard James's voice, gripped her more tightly still. The thud of her heart competed with the precise tick of the second hand from the antique clock in reception. She turned to James suddenly. "One week?"

"Just a week. To check things out. To make sure things are as they should be, and then I'll be off."

She nodded slowly. He'd be going. It would only be for one week. She'd spent ten years without him, growing stronger with each passing day. She could do this. Besides, what was the alternative—a winery owned by someone whose heart lay elsewhere?

"Okay." She'd manage to evade him over the weekend somehow. "I'll meet you at the cafe at seven. If you're sure you won't be bored."

Pete nodded approvingly and stepped aside for James to leave first. But James didn't move straight away. He held her gaze but she refused to look away, despite the blush she could feel rising until her cheeks stung.

"Oh, I doubt we'll be bored. In fact, I'll make sure we won't be."

James only half-listened to Pete as a furiously blushing Susie, muttering excuses, squeezed past them into the winery. He smiled as the smell of machinery oil and lemons wafted over to him. Who'd have thought it could have a stronger effect on his body than the most expensive perfumes? He sighed, glanced briefly at Pete who was giving some last-minute instruction to one of the staff, and then shifted his hungry gaze from Susie's t-shirt, tight over tense shoulders, to her shorts. There, his eyes lingered, admiring her perfectly formed behind. The shorts had definitely seen better days, for which James thanked God. They'd been washed to within an inch of their life and fell in soft folds around her curves. He suddenly had a vivid, visceral recollection of their one night together as lovers. Of how his hands, tentatively at first, had explored her body as their relationship had changed from best friends to lovers.

It hadn't been his first time with a woman, but it might as well have been because the experience had been as different to anything he'd experienced, as winter was to summer. The heat of her skin beneath his fingers had seared deep inside of him, consuming him. He'd felt, what she'd felt; he tasted her as she'd tasted him, they'd become one —complete.

And seeing her now, after all this time, he realized nothing had changed. He still wanted her.

No, there were many words that could describe the next few days but "boring" wouldn't be one of them.

CHAPTER TWO

Susie hesitated at the door of the busy cafe and saw James immediately. He looked incongruous with his expensive suit and perfect good looks in the scruffy cafe, where locals and tourists spilled out onto the terrace. She smoothed down one of the few good dresses she owned and wove her way around the tables, greeting friends as she went. James stood up as she approached.

"You look beautiful, Susie."

"It's Susannah. And no, I don't." She reached over and picked up the wine list. "Have you ordered yet?"

He sat back down, a seductive smile lingering on his lips. "No, I'm old-fashioned like that. I thought I'd wait for you. What do you recommend?"

She cleared her throat and studied the list she knew by heart. "Is our Syrah okay with you?"

"Perfect."

She signaled to the waitress and ordered the wine. Then she took a deep breath. She could do this. She just had to keep it neutral. "So... is this your first visit to the island?"

He grinned, leaned forward, his elbows on the table, supporting a too-intent gaze. "Not to Waiheke, but I've never been to this part of the island before. It's very beautiful." But his eyes were looking at her, not the view.

She swallowed hard, willing a blush not to emerge. She was nearly twenty-eight years old, a professional, and many other things besides, and she could handle meeting an old boyfriend. But this was Mac, Mac, Mac. The name hammered into her head, trying to destroy her hard-won calm. *Be the woman in the video.* She cleared her throat. "Yes, it is." She took another deep breath. "Here on the ridge we've 180 degree views of the Hauraki Gulf, north to the islands and west to Auckland."

His lips twitched as if he knew what she was doing. "Really? Fascinating." He leaned back again in his chair, framed by the rampant vine that clung to the rough-timbered pergola. He looked like a model on a stage set—out of place, transitory. She clung to the thought—he'd get bored, he'd be gone inside a week. She focused on pouring out two glasses of wine, took yet another deep breath and handed him a glass. His fingers brushed hers and she drew back quickly, as if burned. She shot him a dark look and held the glass up to his, in challenge. He swirled and inhaled the wine, nodding appreciatively, before tapping his glass casually against hers.

"Here's to the future of Whisper Creek." He uttered the words like a promise of seduction.

"And may its future be not so very different from its past."

They sipped the deep red wine, without taking their eyes from each other. The low apricot beams of the late sun sparkled in the cut-glass facets of the wineglass, showering his hand with light.

He nodded appreciatively. "It's good. Very good."

"It's 100% syrah from our own grapes. Limited in quantity of course, but the quality's good." She watched with fascination as he swirled the wine around the glass. It took all her restraint not to reach over and run her finger over the flickers of light that played on his hand as it caressed the stem of the wine glass. She remembered the gentle touch of his hand around hers, tugging her into mischief, restraining her from harm. Or mostly. She swallowed. "It's not as important as cabernet sauvignon to us, nor the chardonnay, but it really plays to our strengths—the dryness of the climate, the hot summers..." She trailed off, suddenly aware that the movement of his hand had stopped. She looked up to meet his gaze, the heat in his eyes slamming her defenses back into place. She couldn't let herself get sucked under by his charm. "Are you even listening to me?"

"Of course, Susie. Hanging on every word. Something about wine, I think."

She refused to rise to the bait. "What would you like to eat? I'm afraid we don't have a large selection."

He glanced at the menu and frowned. "So it seems."

She bristled at the implied criticism. "We aim for quality rather than quantity. We focus on in-season specialties."

He leaned forward, his eyes practically stroking her skin until it rose in goose bumps. "Quality is good." His seductive voice sent a sharp tug of desire through her body. "But quality and quantity is better."

She sat bolt upright. "Quality *and* quantity? You're not only talking about the food are you? What kind of changes do you plan to make with the winery? Surely not to increase production by importing grapes from other vineyards?"

"Put it this way, there's room for improvement to the bottom line."

"Bottom line?" Susie sucked in a deep breath, buying time to rein in her temper and her fears. She focused on placing the glass quietly onto the rustic table. "Whisper Creek isn't *about* the bottom line. I've spent the past eight years working here with Pete, building it up from nothing to become a well-regarded boutique winery. And now—"

"You're scared I'll destroy your dreams?"

"Yes."

"They'll disappear anyway unless you pay attention to the profit margin."

"Pete said you didn't intend to make changes."

"Correction. I assured Pete I would neither close down the winery nor amalgamate it with others. I'm sure he wouldn't think it against our terms if I improved it. It doesn't sound like a hanging offense to me. Does it to you?"

"Depends on what you have in mind."

"And that, Susie, depends on what I find when I look around the winery and talk with the staff, tomorrow."

"Okay." She nodded, her mind racing ahead as she planned what to show him, and what to avoid showing him. "I'll show you around the winery tomorrow and you can meet everyone. Then there's The Lodge which is a reasonable earner."

"Ah, The Lodge. The cafe is part of The Lodge's operations, right?" She nodded. "The Lodge could be an extremely *good* earner if done right. Still, I'll reserve judgment until later." He looked around the hectic scene, where it was obvious the waitress couldn't cope. He turned back to her. "We can start with the food. So why don't you choose from the menu for me?"

"Sure." She studied the brief menu. "I suggest the Goat

Cheese and Prosciutto Ravioli to start and the John Dory for main course." She snapped the menu shut. "If that's okay with you?" She placed the order with the harried looking waitress, conscious all the while of his eyes on her, watching her every move.

He swirled his wine around in the glass but his eyes never strayed from hers. "Delicious."

Instinctively she licked her lips, feeling the sensuous sibilance of the word skitter over her skin. Then he turned to ask the waitress for water—which should have already been on the table—and she watched as he flirted with her. Flirted! She glanced away, unable to watch. When he'd been young his charm had been more natural, less obvious. Now, he wielded it like a weapon. And, of course, it worked. Men loved him for his humor and warmth and women loved him for his complete and utter sexiness. Most women, anyway.

She turned back to him, intending to send him a black look but it froze as his gaze caught hers, his eyes caressing her as effectively as if he'd taken her into his arms and held her close. It was hot, encompassing and very, very intimate. Her rational thoughts shattered under the blast of gut-wrenching desire that had nothing to do with reason.

She shook her head. "Don't do that."

He raised his eyebrows. "What is it I'm doing, Susie?"

"It's Susannah, and you're flirting with me."

"I think of you as Susie. And Susie you will stay. Why did you change your name?"

She flicked open the serviette and dropped it onto her lap. "Bad memories. I wanted to start fresh. Besides, Susannah suits me better."

"It doesn't suit the woman I know."

"That woman no longer exists, if she ever did."

"You might be able to fool everyone else but I can see her. Even now. She's there, hiding behind all that businesslike practicality. Do you want to know how I know for sure?"

"I'm sure you're going to tell me anyway."

"Because it's Susie who wants to make quality wines, who doesn't care about profit. No one called Susannah would ignore the balance sheet. It's Susie who has the creative soul."

The sun slipped over the horizon and the evening suddenly shifted into a soft twilight. Words floated, formed sentences and then disappeared before she could speak them. The waitress placed their food in front of them, covering the awkward silence. Then she left the table and the silence fell heavy again. She shook her head.

"You can't deny it, Susie. I remember you, I remember everything."

"Really? I can't." She took a mouthful of the ravioli and hoped the lie was convincing.

"I don't believe you. What about that time we stayed out all night in the tree house at Glencoe?"

The memory of that night, engraved in her heart, flooded her senses. She focused on the salad, buying time. "What about it?" Her voice came out weaker than she'd wanted it to. "Do you like the ravioli?"

He nodded, but his attention wasn't on the food, it was on her. "We spent a lot of time in that tree house."

She took a deep breath and released the tension with a sigh as the memories grew stronger—filling her mind and flooding her with long-repressed feelings of happiness. "Tree house? It was bigger than some of the estate cottages."

"Just as well, given the time we spent there."

An unwilling smile slipped onto her lips. "I remember

you with your hammer and nails. You couldn't stop adding new platforms, building new walls."

"So I did! I'd forgotten about that. I used to like building things. Haven't done that in a long time."

"No, I don't suppose you have."

"Times change but, you know, I've not forgotten those summer evenings that seemed to go on forever. Innocent times."

She scraped her teeth over her lip and looked down and nodded, then swallowed and looked up at him. "They were good times. Apart from when I returned late and got into trouble with Dad."

"You knew you would, and yet you stayed with me. Playing games, talking, or just watching the sun slowly set, keeping me company when I couldn't go home and face *my* father. At least your father never gave you a hiding."

"No, he'd never have done that. And yes, I stayed. Because that's what you do with friends who need you." The sudden darkness of subsequent memories clouded the happy memories. She frowned. "You don't need me now."

The long seconds of silence drew on too long. "Sure. I'm all grown up with no one to beat me up when I get home."

"No one except yourself."

"Oh, Susie. Always the wise one. Always the clever one who thought she could understand more about people than they could understand themselves."

She ignored the sudden bitter tone. She'd hit a raw nerve. It gave her the confidence to ask him the question she needed to know the answer to ever since she'd seen him. "Mac, why are you here?" She didn't know who was most surprised at her use of her old nickname for him. The sudden use of the intimate name jolted them both. His smile didn't reappear.

"I'm looking to secure the future of this winery the best way I can."

She frowned. "I don't understand. Why would you want to do this? At best the profit from the winery would only keep you in pocket money for a few weeks. Why?"

"Because." He sucked in a sharp breath and held it, his eyes narrowing on hers as if looking for some kind of answer.

"Why?" She repeated, more softly, shaking her head.

"Because... I owe you."

"And it's taken ten long years for you to come to this momentous conclusion?"

"It took me ten long years to decide to go against your wishes. Also... I'm beginning a new... *venture* shall we say, next week which will tie up my time. I want to set things straight with you before I embark on it."

"Setting things straight," she repeated. "How? By paying me off?"

"By making sure you have everything you need to carry on, to make sure you can follow the dreams you used to talk about."

"I *had* dreams once—the same as my father's—and you shattered them. That's *so* like you to think you can make my dreams come true now." Her mind, usually so clear and focused, was a fog of suppressed memories and needs. She reached out for her glass but withdrew her hand when she saw how much it shook.

"It's true." He shrugged, almost regretfully. "I can. I know what you want for this winery. And I know how to get it for you."

"And in return, all you want is what? Absolution?

"All?" He asked, his lips curling into a wry grin. "You make it sound as if it were a small thing."

"Small, big. It makes no difference. It's an *impossible* thing. The past happened, you can't make it un-happen. You destroyed my world. You can't remake it."

"I can."

His expression had changed, softened. Maybe it was the light? The twilight has thickened as the low mist that had been threatening all day, blew in from the sea. It filtered into the air all around them, softening the edges of the adobe building, muting the jagged thorns of the bougainvillea and, ironically, *revealing* the face of the boy she once knew.

"How can I trust you after what happened? What's changed?"

"Me," he said quietly.

And for one long moment, she slipped into a trust that she'd felt for him all those years ago. She shook her head, trying to rid it of the phantom feelings. She was imagining things. This was Mac, a man who'd made her destroy a part of herself, and had destroyed her family's future and her trust in the process. She had too much to risk to let herself slide into a nostalgia that made her vulnerable.

"Really?" she said, unable to prevent the sarcasm creeping into her tone. "Really?" she repeated, stronger now. "You've changed, you say? And you think I should welcome this news with open arms, like it's something I've been waiting for my whole life?" The anger and bitterness increased with each word, as her voice grew louder. "You think I should meekly surrender because the charming, handsome James Mackenzie has turned up on my doorstep claiming he's changed?"

"Look, if I could turn the clock back I would."

"And what would you do, huh? *Not* accept the bet from your mate that you could take the virginity of the, what was it he called me, 'the frigid ice queen?'" Her heart was thumping wildly, her control was fracturing with each word but she couldn't stop now. Years of repressed anger spilled to the surface. "*Not* tell me to have that abortion, huh?"

"I didn't tell you to, I suggested—"

"I think I *know* what you said. I was on the other end of the phone, remember? You couldn't even be bothered to come back home to discuss it with me. But then you wouldn't, would you? You had your girlfriend at uni to consider." She pushed away her plate, unable to eat another mouthful.

He closed his eyes as if he'd been struck. His lips pressed together in an expression of something like regret.

"And then there was my father," she continued. "His dreams of leasing Glencoe land for a winery, shattered when your mother forced us off the estate. He was distraught, otherwise he'd never have had that accident. No, Mac, it doesn't work like that. I've not forgiven and I've not forgotten and I certainly don't trust you."

He also pushed away his half-eaten dinner. "So it would seem. But..." He turned to face her, the mist muting his glamour, revealing the shadows and subtleties, the changes ten years had wrought. "Trust isn't required for me to make sure I'm satisfied with all aspects of my investment."

"The winery's in good shape. I'll show you around tomorrow. There's a ferry at five you can catch." She looked around to discover that the cafe was nearly empty. She jumped up. "I... I have to go."

He caught up to her on the edge of the verandah, his hand restraining her from descending the steps. She refused to look at him. Instead focusing on the gnarled olive trees, that emerged grotesque from the sea mist and the line of muslin-covered grapevines growing ever more indistinct. The silence deepened, moved somehow away from accusation, and sank into an unrelenting heaviness.

"I'm with you for a week. Get used to the idea. I'm going nowhere until that week is up. And that, Susie, is something you're going to have to accept. Trust or not."

"You're being under-handed, Mac. You're forcing me to be with you. Doesn't sound like you've changed at all. You're still coercing people in order to get what you want."

"I do what I have to do."

"The end has always justified the means with you hasn't it? Back at Glencoe, you made me believe you were in love with me to win the bet. Here, now, you buy the winery in order to force your way into my world."

"That's not how it *was*. That's not how it *is*."

Grief welled up over what might have been and what she'd lost. She stepped away, shaking his arm off hers. "You must go, Mac, you *must*. I can't do this."

He didn't move. "Ten years ago I left you, when I shouldn't have done. I'm not going to make the same mistake again. I'll leave at the end of the week and not before."

She shivered as the mist thickened, casting a veil over the outside lights of the cafe. She felt she was drowning in a darkness from which it had taken her years to emerge. "And do I have any choice in this?"

"No," he said lightly. "Unless you want to shoot Pete's future down into flames, taking yours with it. No, you don't. Now, you'll walk home and I'll walk beside you at a respectable distance. Okay?"

She nodded. It would have to be. He was right, she had no choice.

. . .

In front of them the darkness was punctuated by lamps whose dispersed halos lit the twists of the path that led down to the beach and her cottage.

She didn't want to, but she couldn't resist stealing glances at him every time they passed one of the solar lamps. The first light revealed a head bent, looking away from her, down to the path, as if lost in thought. Then, a few more paces later she glanced at him and briefly met his gaze. She could feel its heat even in the mist that robbed everything of color.

She stopped at the point where the path descended steeply down onto the beach. Below them stood her cottage, just above the sand. They were out of the reach of the lights and darkness slid all around them. There was only the sound of the cicadas, quieter now, in the trees behind them, and the sea surging up the beach and dragging the fine sand down again, into its depth.

"It's small, but it's home," she said pointing down to the utilitarian 1940s cottage that had none of the decorative features of earlier colonial cottages.

"It suits you."

"Small and featureless?"

"Susie." He sighed. "Why do you insist on taking everything I say the wrong way. You know I don't mean that. I mean it's beautiful. Look at it. The porch, the chair facing the ocean—it's a perfect retreat."

"A retreat. Yes, I suppose it is." She hadn't thought of it in those terms before. She'd always prided herself on being a realist. But Mac was right. She'd made a place where she thought no one could get to her.

"How long have you lived here?"

"I moved to the island around eight years ago. What with Mum and Dad gone, and my brother traveling, I needed work and picking grapes was all I knew."

"What about university?"

"Never happened. No money."

"I'm sorry. You'd have done well."

She chewed her lip, irritated. She refused to be pitied. She'd never been into self-pity. "I did well without it."

He stepped back and looked around. "You're right. You have."

"Yes, I have. Pete could see what a work horse I was and so let me train up in the business. And I rent the house from the estate. I don't earn much and the house is a bit of a wreck but I like it. It's home." She gave him a sweeping gaze —from his expensive leather shoes, to his stylish shirt and perfectly trimmed dark hair. "But I doubt you *really* think this is the height of perfection."

He frowned and didn't speak for a few moments. "It's what you used to want, and you have it. That's achievement in my book."

There was something wistful in his words that touched her. "And do you have what you used to want, Mac?"

"What do you think?"

"I think you've followed your dreams, you've reached them, and now you're wondering if you followed the right ones."

She saw the barrier fall instantly. It was like a shiny veneer of protection. She understood. She knew all about protection.

"Ah, so wise. You think you know me so well. You think I've turned up here to appease my conscience, finding my dreams hollow. Well, Susie, you're partly right and partly wrong. I've had a ball. And I'll continue to have a ball. We only get one life and I'm playing it hard. But that doesn't make me a total jerk. I'm here to make reparation and then I'll be gone." He stepped away from her, back to the path. "Goodnight, Susie."

"Goodnight, Mac.

"Tomorrow morning. We'll meet at nine."

"Sure."

She continued down the path to her cottage and, in the instant before she turned on the outside light, glanced up at him. He'd paused by a light, and was looking down at her. She flicked on the outside light—flooding the front steps, the rough marram grass and sand dunes around it—casting him into shadow. This was how it *had* to be—him on the outside.

CHAPTER THREE

Out of the corner of her eye Susie watched James enter the foyer. She continued to chat to an early-morning visitor to the winery. Eventually the visitor moved next door to the tasting area, leaving Susie and James alone. Susie walked over to where James was riffling through the visitor information brochures.

"Looking for something in particular?"

He flicked through the bundle of brochures in his hands. "I was looking to see what luxury lodges there were on the island."

"There aren't any. Didn't you sleep well?" It was meant to have been a polite question but, for some reason, it sounded far too personal. James looked up at her with dark blue eyes that were full of innuendo.

"No, I didn't." He dropped the brochures onto the over-sized oak table. They scattered untidily. "You?"

"Fine thanks. Never better." Susie tried to cover her lie by immediately tidying up the brochures he'd displaced. But she doubted she'd succeeded, Mac had always been able to see straight through her.

"Is that right? Then what was your light doing on at four this morning?"

"And what were you doing spying on me?"

"I went for a very early morning walk. Thought if I couldn't sleep I may as well enjoy the garden in the moonlight. The mist had cleared by then and I could see your cottage."

She shrugged as she deposited the last of the brochures into the display rack, not wanting to look him in the eye, not wanting to give away even an inkling of her feelings during the night. Of how she'd lain awake, hot and wanting, and knowing that her body could never have what it craved. Not without risking everything she'd earned. James *had* to be out of bounds. "Probably dozed off with it on."

"Yeah, right." He came closer to her. "Want to know why I couldn't sleep? Want to know what I was thinking of?"

"Not particularly." She wanted to step away—his gaze was too penetrating, too personal and intrusive. She still refused to meet his eye. "But if you want to tell me then I'm sure I won't be able to stop you."

He reached out and touched her and she stilled immediately. His touch ignited a heat and a deep need for him to touch her again that shocked her. She tried to force herself to turn away but was rooted to the spot. Her body reacted despite what her mind told her to do. And her mind was quite clear. Run. Get out of there. *Right now*. She didn't move.

His gaze slipped to her mouth, as his thumb shifted up her chin and moved along her lower lip. She swallowed and kept her lips firmly pressed together to stop the trembling that threatened to give her away. He tilted her chin so she was forced to look at him.

"It wasn't what I was *thinking*, Susie, that kept me awake. It was what I was *feeling*. The same as you, judging by your reaction to my touch."

The heat in his eyes threatened to destroy her. She inhaled deeply, willing her body to calm. "Stop this, Mac. We've work to do. Whatever you think, or feel, I don't want this. This is business only."

"You're fooling yourself."

"I do whatever I have to do to stay safe. End of story. Now, I assume you still want to look around the winery you've just bought? Or do you think you're looking at your new possession right now? Is it me you think you own?"

Much to her consternation he grinned and he didn't move his hand. "Now, there's a thought. Owning Susie. Tell me, would you like to be owned?"

She shouldn't have hesitated but his touch did things to her that her mind had no ability to counteract. The word "owned" conjured up images that made her melt from the inside out. She slapped down his hand. "Don't be ridiculous."

"Too little, too late. I *know* you. I know you like the thought of us together."

"You can think what you like." She swallowed. "Let's get on with it, shall we? Business. That's all." She opened an inner door and the rattle of bottles being carried by a forklift grew louder. "I'll show you around the winery." She could do it. Focus on the business, keep a physical distance between them, make excuses not to be alone with him because she simply couldn't trust herself.

"Fine. Today the winery and tomorrow..." He walked up to her and tilted his head towards hers. "There's the weekend."

Susie winced inwardly. She had to get him to leave

before the weekend. It was bad enough fending Mac off, without the added emotional pressure of seeing him with Tom. "You'll be bored at the weekend. You'd be better off going to Auckland and returning here Monday if you really insist."

He just grinned, a pleasant but very determined grin. "No. I'll stay here for the weekend, get to know the place better."

She sighed and forced her face into a tight, even more determined smile. "Sure. No problem." And there wouldn't be. She'd made sure she and Tom would be too busy to see anything of James. Just the thought of seeing these two people together sent her heart racing. If James thought he'd be able to force his company on her this weekend, he had another think coming. "I'll show you the winery and then show you around the island."

Susie slammed her foot on the accelerator, taking out her frustration on the old jeep and causing James to brace himself into his seat as they bounced along the rough track. The sight of his white knuckles gripping the door handle gave her grim satisfaction. She accelerated up to the bend beyond which the edge of the cliff lay—it was a spectacular view and an equally spectacularly scary road—and turned sharply. She glanced at James again and couldn't help grinning as he briefly closed his eyes before turning his narrowed gaze to her.

"So what do you think?" She shouted above the revving engine as she skidded over the juddering ruts of the rough road.

"I think you're driving hasn't improved."

"About the winery." She changed into a higher gear to give her the control she needed to round another hairpin bend, smiling to herself as Mac was thrown against the door.

"Small but beautifully made."

She stopped the jeep in a cloud of dust, at a vantage point near the cliff top. "So nothing to change then?"

"I didn't say that."

And she knew it. As they'd been going round the winery she'd seen it through his eyes, from the machinery which needed updating, to the lack of polish in the public wine-tasting areas. But a new lodge it did not need.

She pulled on the handbrake and sat back, and watched as James jumped out of the jeep and turned 360 degrees, taking in the unrivaled views. To the east, dark, dense forests covered the rocky terrain, to the south, vineyards raked the land and, to the north and west, the pristine beaches swept around them, fringing the Hauraki Gulf where islands faded in and out of the soft blue haze.

She followed him but went further out to the edge of the cliff and sat down, her legs dangling over the near vertical drop. James didn't join her. She looked back to him. "Care to elaborate?"

"Not sitting there, I don't."

She grinned as she looked out to sea. "You never did like heights."

"Is that why you brought me here, then? Some kind of small way to torture me?"

She grinned to herself but managed to hide it before she turned back to him. "It's a good place to look around and see how beautiful it is. To see"—she peered at him over her sunglasses—"how unique it is, how natural and unspoiled it is."

"And *how*, I suppose you're saying, it should remain so."

"Well, you can't think otherwise, looking at this, can you?"

He walked up behind her. "I don't want to spoil anything, Susie, that's not what I'm here for. I want to leave things better than they were."

She swallowed and stared out, unblinking at the horizon until her eyes watered. "Okay. Some of the machinery needs updating. I'm sure you noticed that. And we don't have the marketing expertise we need to earn money from a limited vintage."

"My friend Guy, who owns Onihau Winery and Lodge, can help you there. Next week, I'm going to Onihau. Come with me and we can discuss his marketing strategies, as well as check out his hospitality business."

She was torn. She wanted the carrot James was dangling in front of her. It was what she'd been working towards after all. But it would mean spending time with him and his friends, it would threaten the impregnable wall she'd built around herself to keep herself strong, keep herself isolated.

"Do I have any choice in this?"

He sighed. "Of course you do. But you know it makes sense. What are you so scared of? Me?"

"You *wish*."

"Do you remember how we used to dare each other?"

She smiled but made sure not to let him see. "Sure. I used to dare you to climb up to the tor."

He shook his head. "I hated that. It was so high. But I did it. And *you*, I used to dare you to go walk into the pub and talk to people."

"And I did that and hated every minute of it."

"So...I *dare* you to come to the Wairarapa, to Onihau."

"We're not fourteen years old any longer, Mac."

"Come on. What happened to the old Susie who'd never back down from a dare?"

He was doing it, he was getting to her, just like he wanted to. She banged the heel of her boot against the chalk face of the cliff in irritation, dislodging some stones. She jumped as a firm hand clamped down on her shoulder. "Do *not*, do *that*, Susie. I don't want to have to become a hero and rescue you from half way down a cliff."

She couldn't help grinning at the thought and felt a flare of the old devilment that he'd always sparked in her as a child. She kicked her heel against the cliff again. "Now, that's something I'd like to see."

He shot her a warning look. "No way."

An idea—stupid and yet compelling—slid into her mind. "Tell you what, if I accept your dare of coming to the Wairarapa with you, then you'll have to accept a dare from me."

"Now who's being juvenile?"

She laughed. "Oh, yes, that's right, it's juvenile if *you* don't want to do something."

He sighed, scuffed the tufting grass under his shoes and then looked up from under a lowered brow with suspicious eyes. "Fair point. Okay. What is it you want me to do?"

She jumped up, hands on hips and nodded to a place where a narrow path ducked down off the top of the cliff and followed a rocky ledge along to a protruding rock, surrounded by nothing but air on three sides with the cliff face behind. "See that rock that sticks out over there? That's where I like to sit sometimes, look out across the ocean, at the waves, the birds soaring close by, watching passing whales. Dare you."

He shook his head. "You, *woman,* are evil. You know full well I never could stand heights."

"It wouldn't be a challenge if it was easy."

He laughed but the laughter died on his lips as he looked at the sheer drop down into the sea. "Jeez..." The word slid from his lips as if someone had punched him in the gut.

"Mac, you owe me..."

"Okay." His voice was even despite the fact he felt a wave of nausea rise up. He swallowed it down. He took a step towards the cliff edge and decided to play on her brief look of concern. He stretched out his hand and gripped hers. She didn't push it away.

"Scared, are we?" she teased.

"What do you think?" He didn't care what she thought, so long as she didn't take her hand away. He followed her, edging his feet along the stony ledge to a place where the ledge was wider and sloped backwards. "This is madness. You're not even looking where you're going!"

She turned to him and grinned. "I know it well, I can feel the path with my feet. Come on." He edged a step further and stopped, but there was an intensity in her eyes, a sort of defiant urging, that he couldn't ignore.

It was as if she wanted to see how far he'd go, how far he'd follow her. She didn't smile just held his gaze with that look of old. It worked. He followed her until he was standing beside her on a wider ledge. Her expression changed then.

"You're not afraid."

He wasn't looking at the view. He had eyes only for her. "Not any more."

She looked away quickly, as if confused and sat down

on the ledge. He leaned against the rock face with assumed nonchalance. No way was he going to sit and dangle his feet over the ledge like her. Gulls soared high in front of them, suspended by the updraft. He might have mastered his fear of heights to a manageable degree but he hadn't felt so terrified in a long time. Nor had he felt so alive. "You really know how to show a man a good time, Susie."

She laughed and he could hear the exhilaration in her voice. "You mean I know how to scare the heck out of them!"

"Is that why you haven't got a man in your life?"

The smile faded instantly and she turned to him. "Why do you presume that? You don't know anything about my life now. I could have a string of men for all you know."

"Do you?"

He immediately regretted his words when her expression softened. He looked away, as if not seeing her would stop him from hearing her answer. "I have... someone."

Her words were too brief, too unrevealing and ambiguous, but they stung nevertheless. She didn't need him, she didn't want him. He felt breathless, winded, and it was totally unexpected. All Pete had mentioned was that Susie was single. Otherwise, he'd been unforthcoming about any of his staff's personal life and he hadn't pressed his enquiries. Now, to find there was someone after all blindsided him. A wave of nausea swept over him that had nothing to do with vertigo. Twenty-four hours and she'd slipped under his skin again and he hadn't even realized it.

"This 'Tom' I heard Pete mention?"

Susie nodded her head but didn't elaborate.

"I think we should go. I'll catch the evening ferry and meet up with friends in Auckland tonight." He sighed. "I'll see you Monday at the airport to go to Onihau."

"Sure." She fished a phone from her shorts and quickly sent a text. "I've ordered a taxi for you."

Her relief was almost palpable and it destroyed any sense of enjoyment he'd gained from the afternoon. He gestured for her to go ahead of him and watched her pass, trying to decipher the firm set of her lips. He focused on her words, still fighting the terror of walking along a narrow ledge, so high above the pounding sea. Damn it. Okay she wanted the weekend but he wasn't giving up so easily. He'd be back and next week would be on his terms. "So you have the weekend in which to clear your calendar for the next week."

She climbed back up to the cliff top and they returned to the jeep. "It's already clear."

"The 'someone' isn't too demanding then?"

"Oh, yes, he's pretty demanding. But I only see him weekends."

"Right, so that leaves the week for me, then. Perfect." They approached the jeep and he reached around her and opened the door for her.

"For you? For the business, you mean?"

"One and the same. You accepted the dare, remember?"

"I must have been mad. One brief risk of vertigo against long days with you and your friends."

"Come on. That cliff was perilous. One false step and I'd have been history."

"You know, Mac? It feels pretty much the same for me."

Her words echoed in his head as they drove back in silence. Was he really such a threat to her? It was so the opposite of how he wanted her to feel. But he hadn't come here to revive her feelings for him, had he? He'd come here to secure her future, make sure she was all right before he moved on to another chapter of his own life. That was all.

Pay his dues and move on. The fact she had a man in her life *shouldn't* matter to him at all. Particularly when *his* future plans most definitely didn't include her.

They turned into the winery, nestled on its ridge-top site in front of a stand of original bush, and she pulled up beside a dusty car.

"There's your taxi." They watched in silence as the taxi driver stepped out of The Lodge, carrying James's bags to the taxi. "You were packed already?"

"I'm always prepared to move on. That's what I do best." He jumped out the jeep and walked up to her as she slowly got out the car. She stood holding onto the jeep door as if for defense. He watched the fall of her bright hair flick in the breeze and just managed to restrain his hand from sliding down its silky length. "Okay. So we'll meet at the airport Monday, as arranged."

"Sure. Monday, then."

She continued to stand, guarded by the jeep door, as he got into the taxi. He didn't turn around to look at her as they drove off. He couldn't. Just twenty-four hours earlier he'd arrived wanting to put things right between them so he could move forward with his plans. So he could do the right thing, clear up the one thing that had continued to haunt him and blight his future. But he was leaving more deeply enmeshed in Susie than before. He'd wondered if things had changed. And they had, but not in the way he'd anticipated. He wanted her more than ever. And she wanted him less than ever. And it was too late for either of them.

He shifted his head slightly and watched her grow smaller through the wing mirror, until she was just a dot, a dot that refused to disappear when he closed his eyes. Too late? He couldn't bear the thought of it. It was never too late. He had to go back to her. Other man, or no other man. Trust or no trust.

She watched the taxi disappear out of sight, dust rising in a cloud behind it. She felt empty as she walked down to the jetty to wait for the mail boat to arrive. Empty and confused. She'd wanted him gone and yet she felt as if he'd taken a part of her with him. Her heart was heavy. Seeing him again had brought back so many thoroughly repressed memories that it hurt. Like releasing a tourniquet that had been kept tight for too long, the blood surged into that unused area causing pain.

She squinted into the horizon, watching the mail boat pass round the promontory to the small jetty at the opposite end of the bay from her cottage. She could just about see a wave from the front of the boat. She waved back, a grin spreading across her face as a surge of love swept through her. It was always like this when he came.

"Stop the car."

The driver looked at James through the rear view mirror but didn't say anything and stopped the car dead. The engine continued to run and the air conditioning blasted out its chill air. But it couldn't cool down James's feelings. He'd always been driven by his feelings, *always*. He'd never had a cool head and it had got him into no end of trouble. And he felt the familiar feeling again, but he couldn't ignore it. He was leaving behind more than he was moving towards.

He slumped back in the seat as he realized what he was about to do. "Turn around. Take me back to the winery."

He leaned forward. "Better still, drop me off at the bay and wait for me there."

The taxi parked at the bend before the rise that revealed the small bay and valley of the winery. James walked down the dusty road to the bay, wondering, with each step, what he was going to say to her. She'd made it clear she wanted him gone. Too clear. Why had she been so adamant when he'd seen the opposite message in every gesture, every small smile, every flash of heat in her eyes?

He heard the sound of a motorboat speed away and frowned. It was very hot. The heat of the day hung suspended, heavy and unmoving in the calm air. When he reached the turn in the bend he stopped abruptly. He frowned into the bright light, trying to see more clearly. He raised his sunglasses. She was with someone. She was walking towards the cottage with her arm casually draped around a young boy. What the hell? He knew her brother, Iain, hadn't had any children, so there were no nephews. A friend's child probably. He must have just been dropped off the boat that was disappearing around the headland. James frowned. Who was he? A friend's son? A relative? The boy looked about, what? Ten? He didn't have a clue about children, but the boy wasn't a child and wasn't yet a teenager. Somewhere around ten, he estimated. Dark hair, much like his own. Going to be tall if his gangly limbs said anything about him. He remembered going through the same stage himself. Yes, definitely not a teenager yet. Though, by the look of the size of his feet, the boy would grow to be about as tall as him.

It all added up to something that suggested Susie had been lying to him. James strode forward. He had no idea what was going on or why Susie had lied to him, but he was damn sure he was going to find out.

. . .

Susie watched with amusement as Tom peered into the fridge. There's a meat pie for you. I thought you'd be hungry."

He grinned over the fridge door. "I'm always hungry." He took a mouthful of pie. "So how's your week been, Susie?"

She rolled her eyes. "Mum. Call me Mum."

"Nah, it's cool to call your mum by their first name, they all do it at school."

She sighed. "Okay, fine. The week's been good really, I guess. The winery's safe. Pete's sold to a new investor who wants us to carry on more or less as we have been doing."

"Brilliant." She smiled. Her son was so sweet. Just like his father. She knew he was too young to really understand the implications of the deal but there'd always just been the two of them and their circumstances had made them closer than the usual mother-son relationship.

There was a knock at the door. She froze. She wasn't expecting anyone. She always kept this time free for family.

"I'll get it." Tom started to walk over to the door.

She put out her hand. "No, it's okay, Tom, you eat, I'll get it."

She walked down the sunny yellow hallway, past the cluttered coat rack and saw a man's shape through the glass door. She paused briefly to gather herself. She took a deep breath and opened the door.

Gone was the smile, gone was the charm. James stood, frowning, his jacket hooked over his finger, his other hand in his pocket.

"Mac! What are you doing here? Did you forget something?"

"Can I come in?"

She glanced behind her. Tom was quietly eating in the kitchen.

"I'll come out." She slipped the door closed behind her. "Let's walk and you can tell me what's on your mind."

He raised his eyebrows. "Sure." She grabbed a wrap from the coat rack and stepped out onto the worn verandah. The sea breeze was picking up as evening descended. He followed her down the steps and fell into step beside her on the scrunchy sand.

"So what's up? Did you leave something at The Lodge?"

"No."

Her heart beat more rapidly as she watched him look down at the sand thoughtfully.

"Plane delayed?"

"Not that either." He put his hand on her arm and she came to an abrupt stop. "I needed to know why you wanted me gone so quickly."

She shook her head. "What do you mean?"

"Suse, you were never good at pretending to be anything other than you are, why try now?"

"Because I need to, Mac. I need it for protection."

His frown deepened. "From me?"

She nodded. Suddenly there was a shout from behind them and Tom appeared, bounding towards them with a surfboard under his arm. Susie dragged the shawl around her more tightly and smiled at Tom. "Careful out there."

Tom grinned and came to a halt in a spray of sand in front of them.

James returned his grin and Susie held her breath. "Aren't you going to introduce us, Suse?"

Tom stepped forward. "I'm Tom."

"And I'm James. Nice to meet you, Tom." James met the boy's extended hand and gripped it in a firm shake. "You live round here?"

"Weekends. I go to school in Auckland now though."

"Tom's staying the weekend." She smiled at Tom. "It's a non-stop food-fest."

"Yeah, Susie likes to spoil me. But I tell her jokes in return."

Susie watched Tom's words have an effect on James. The fact that Tom didn't call her "Mum" came as a relief. She felt an overwhelming need to keep her personal life very personal. She needed to keep the barriers up because James threatened to demolish them with every passing hour she was with him. Why didn't he just go and leave her like he was always going to do, like he always would do? Why prolong the inevitable?

James nodded slowly as if considering everything Tom said carefully. "It's good to be spoiled sometimes."

"But not all the time." Susie couldn't help saying pointedly to James, who'd been spoiled rotten by his mother growing up. She turned to Tom. "Tom, why don't you go and get your swim and then I'll fix us something to eat."

"Are you staying for dinner, sir?"

"I haven't been invited."

"Of course James is welcome to stay but..." She turned to James. "He has to be off. Won't even stay for a cup of tea, will you?"

"Cup of tea's not my thing, thanks Susie."

"Nor mine!" Tom laughed. "Nice to meet you, sir." They watched him run off, the rope of the surfboard trailing in the sand, before he threw himself into the sea and slammed his body onto the surfboard and paddled out.

"He's got good manners."

"Better than yours at his age." She could see what James was thinking and the unspoken question hung between them. She followed his gaze to Tom, who was sizing up an incoming wave. "So, why have you come back? Surely it's nothing that can't be dealt with over the phone."

"I wanted to know what you were hiding. You weren't telling me everything." He glanced back at Tom. "And now I can see why."

"You think it's because of Tom."

"Isn't it?"

There was a yell and Tom stumbled up the beach towards them a wide grin. "Did you see that one?"

She turned to the boy and her heart contracted. She shook her head. "Sorry."

"Jeez, Susie." For the second time, she was glad of the name he called her. "Are you coming in for a swim, sir?"

James shook his head.

"Mac—I mean James—is just leaving," she found herself saying. Then she wished she hadn't as James turned slowly towards her, a world of meaning on his face. All the chat and flirtation of the day had vanished and in their place were words—a question—he seemed hesitant to ask. She bit her lip. She sure as hell wasn't going to volunteer an answer.

"Maybe later."

"Cool!" Tom raced back down the beach once more.

James gazed steadily at Susie.

"Later?" she asked quietly.

"Sure." His eyes searched hers. "I'm going back to The Lodge. I'll stay the weekend then we can fly to the Wairarapa on Monday together."

Her heart slammed into her chest. Business was one thing but a weekend in close proximity to James? She couldn't do it. "But I thought I was going to meet up with you at the airport?"

"Change of plan." He shot her a grim look and walked away.

Susie sucked in a long slow breath, as she watched him leave, desperate to quiet the rapid beating of her heart. James was nearly at the road when Tom called out. "Susie!" She couldn't take her eyes off James, still wondering what was running through his mind. "Mum!" Tom called again. Susie closed her eyes and turned to Tom who cupped his hands around his mouth and gave another yell, so loud it could be heard all around the small crescent of the bay. "Mum! Did you see that one?"

She shook her head stiffly in reply to Tom, who then dived into the water. She didn't move. Just waited. Waited for the sound of James's taxi to turn around and roar back up the dusty, rough road to the winery. Waited for the drone of the engine as it juddered across the worn corners of the road. But there was nothing. Only the ebb and flow of the waves on the brilliant white sand, and the clatter of the Phoenix palm at the bottom of the garden where the sand dunes began.

She had to know if James had heard. She turned around slowly. He stood there, closer than she'd imagined, watching her. He didn't say a word. He didn't need to. She knew what he was thinking.

CHAPTER FOUR

J ames felt winded, his mind numb, his suspicions confirmed. Tom was *not* a friend's child, *not* a relative, *not* just some kid. He was *her* son!

Susie stood, equally still, facing him, her eyes bright, biting her lip. She almost looked nervous.

"I've changed my mind. I will have a cup of tea and dinner after all."

She looked down at the sandy ground and nodded. "Sure. I'll go and put the kettle on." She disappeared inside while James strode up the hill, back to the taxi, two words repeating themselves as he went—*her son, her son*. He walked in time to them and was aware *only* of them as he distractedly told the taxi driver to take his bags back to The Lodge. He didn't go back inside the house to Susie immediately but stood on the dunes behind the house, looking out over the beach to where Tom was wading through the shallows. Tom turned and waved, a huge grin splitting his face. Then he turned back and waded out into deeper water.

James closed his eyes against the ferocity of the low sun but he could still see the boy's face. The boy was Susie's son but who was the father? Could it be him? Could it be that Susie never had that abortion after all?

He let the hope that he had a son slowly fill his senses. A son. It was something he'd never thought to have, not since the consequences of that hot night in the hayloft. Because, long afterwards, his guilt had made him do something stupid, something irrevocable, something to punish himself. But it had been only much later that he'd realized he'd never be able to atone for what he'd done to Susie.

He opened his eyes and watched as Tom jumped the waves, waiting for the rolling wave that was gathering power further out. His dark hair was like James's, thick and almost black. His shoulders promised to be broad but his body was skinny and long.

Was the boy his? Was James's instinct about the boy true? When James had first seen him, his gangly limbs, his coloring, his approximate age, he'd felt a slam of recognition. But perhaps that was just because he remembered being a boy like him? Or perhaps it was because of something more? Had Susie purposely not told him about Tom because she didn't want him to know that Tom was his son?

Secrets. He never could stand them. From his days growing up in a household of deceit and barely-suppressed anger, he'd hated them. He wasn't leaving until he'd got to the bottom of this one.

He watched as Tom took the wave and slid far up the shore towards him. With a cry of delight he picked up his surfboard and came bounding up to James, spraying water as he shook his hair.

"You're staying for dinner after all, sir?"

"Yeah. I decided I needed to hear your jokes."

"Cool. The girls love them."

James groaned inwardly at evidence of further similarity between them as he followed Tom up the worn wooden steps to the cottage where Susie was busily moving around the kitchen. She brought out a cup of hot chocolate and a cup of tea and placed them carefully onto the table. She caught James's gaze but turned away suddenly and James could hear her banging around in the kitchen. He sat back onto the flat cushions, embroidered with homely motifs that lined the antique cane chair. Tom might like him being there, but he could hear from Susie's impatient movements that his mother wasn't happy. At the first opportunity he'd ask her. But, until then, he'd enjoy the luxury of imagining he had a son, something he'd thought to be impossible. Until now. He might, just might, have been given a second chance.

Susie picked up the saucepan lid that had fallen to the wooden floor with a clatter, and jerked the heavy pan back onto the stove. She knew what he was thinking. It was written all over his face. He may be a bastard but he'd always been utterly incapable of lying to save his life.

"Tom! Come and lay the table!"

"But, I was just showing—"

"Tom!"

"Sure, Susie." Tom planted a kiss on her cheek, hearing her irritation. She grunted, unwilling to show how well his display of affection had worked. He shunted the pile of books and papers up to one end of the scrubbed pine table and retrieved the willow-pattern plates from the dresser.

As Susie took the casserole from the oven, she turned and saw James leaning against the door jamb, silently watching them both. "It's just beef casserole. No frills."

"Smells great. And I'm sure it'll taste great too."

"Susie's cooking is always good. Pete reckons her cooking is better than The Lodge."

"Is that so?"

She sat down, the wooden chair scraping against the bare floor boards. "Last night at the Lodge, the service wasn't normal. If our other waitress's mother hadn't been sick, the service would have been top notch, as usual."

"I'm sure it would have been," he said smoothly. "I hope her mother is better now?"

"Yes," she said slightly mollified. "Much better."

"That's good. It bodes well for dinner tomorrow night then."

She glared at him. She knew what he was saying. You can't run a restaurant on a shoestring. And he was right.

"So, Tom, tell me about school. What do you enjoy most?"

"Soccer."

James grinned. "Not Science, or English or Math then?"

Tom pulled a face and hastily looked at Susie. "It's not that I don't like them. Just that, well soccer's real fun. We play at lunch—"

"I hope you eat the lunches your aunt packs for you," Susie said.

"I eat that at morning tea. I buy chips for lunch."

Susie shook her head in despair. "Tom's an eating machine."

"So I see." James smiled. "You're going to be tall, like your father?"

Tom shrugged his angular shoulders and looked at Susie. "Was Dad tall, Susie?"

Color filled her cheeks. "Yes." She jumped up to fill a glass of water. "Anyone else like a glass of water?" She let the water run as she gripped the edge of the butler's sink, willing James not to continue that line of conversation.

She heard a chair scrape behind her and he was beside her. She turned to him warily. His eyes were full of questions. But, instead, he held out a glass. "That would be fine... For now."

She knew she wasn't going to escape without a grilling. But not while Tom was there.

After dinner Susie insisted on doing the washing up, a job that was usually Tom's. She didn't want to risk being alone with James, didn't want him asking questions she'd prefer not to answer. The past had been traumatic enough without revisiting it.

There was a shout from the living room. Susie edged towards the open door, making sure she kept to the shadows. The soft glow from the sidelights revealed a scene that nearly made her cry out. She raised her fist to her mouth and watched as Tom and James concentrated hard on a board game, at which it appeared Tom was winning. They sat cross-legged on the floor, their absorbed faces looking up from time to time trying to catch each other out, hands reaching out to the board to move their pieces. Then a whoop of glee from Tom again.

"I own it! With hotels! $2,000 please, James." He held out his hand triumphantly as James was forced to resort to the dwindling pile of $10s and $1s.

"*You* are a hard opponent."

"Well, you should have put a hotel on Mayfair when you had the chance."

James grinned and rolled the dice.

How likely was it that James *wouldn't* have put a hotel

on such an expensive property, Susie wondered. He was obviously going easy on Tom. But then, James had always been like that hadn't he? Gentle, kind and always sensitive to the needs of others. Other people beside herself, obviously.

"And you reckon you're not good at this game? I'd hate to play you at soccer, something you reckon you *are* good at."

Tom knelt up in his excitement. "Let's have a game of soccer tomorrow. Yeah?"

James looked across to where Susie thought she was standing undetected.

"No. I'm sure *James*"—she emphasized his given name —"has other plans. He's only here for a few days."

He pushed himself off the floor. "No, no plans. That would be great."

"Choice! Soccer it is. And you can come to our picnic. We're sailing round to the bay. Can't he, Mum?" Her young son's brows suddenly furrowed as he realized he might be asking something she didn't want to happen.

It broke her heart to see how he'd taken to James, how starved of male company he was. Pete did his best but he had another life, away from the island, and now his focus had switched further afield, to the Mackenzie Country. Tom was of an age where he really responded to men, where he needed a man's solid guidance. But she couldn't allow him to get close to James who'd be gone within days. It would be too painful to watch Tom wondering why James hadn't called, just as she had all those years ago.

She stepped into the light, strengthened by the reminder and shook her head. "No, I'm sure James has other plans. He won't want to come out with us." She shot James a warning look. "Will you, James?"

"Actually, I would. I can't think of anything I'd like better."

"Really?" She said archly. "Cold sausage rolls, potato chips—"

"Salt and vinegar?"

"Yes!" Tom shouted.

"Love them," added James.

"Meat paste sandwiches—"

"Paste?" asked James faintly.

"Paste," she replied firmly. "Tom's favorite. Probably with a sprinkling of sand because you know how *that* gets everywhere."

"Indeed."

Susie grimaced at James's wicked smile. "And lemonade. Probably flat by the time we get there."

"Cold gritty food and flat lemonade. My favorites."

Tom gave James a high five. "And soccer."

"It'll be a perfect day, then."

"And night," added Susie, saving her big guns until last. "Didn't Tom tell you? We're camping under the stars tomorrow night." It took Susie all her self-control not to laugh out loud at how quickly James's face fell. James had only gone camping with her once when they were barely into their teens and had sworn never to do it again. And she had no doubt that he'd kept to that. Until now.

"Camping." He took a deep intake of breath. "Well... camping. That..."

"Will be brilliant!" finished off Tom, who could scarcely contain his excitement.

James nodded as if urging himself on to some kind of enthusiasm. "Yes. Yes, it will."

"Hot drink before you go?" Susie smiled sweetly, enjoying James's discomfort. She wanted James off the island, didn't she? Well, what better way than to show him how utterly unable he would be to fit in here.

James stood up and stretched. "Thank you but no. I'd better get going. I think I'll need a good night's sleep."

"To make up for the one you're not going to get tomorrow night?"

"Exactly."

"Yes, he *will* get a good night's sleep tomorrow, Susie. We *always* sleep well outside. It'll be great, James. The weather's clear, we can look at the stars and tell stories."

Susie made a mistake then, of looking at James. There was nothing between their gaze except memories: memories of a time when the two of them had been young and innocent and had lain side by side in the sweet grasses of the high Mackenzie Country and watched as the long dusk had given way to a night sky full of stars. They'd taken it in turns to talk about their dreams, their hopes, their stories.

"Oh..." Susie gasped and turned away abruptly, scared James would see how much the poignant memory affected her.

"We'll be leaving early because of the tide. Will you go swimming? How about cricket? Did you play cricket when you were young?" Tom continued to bombard James with questions and Susie slipped away, unable to face James again.

She grabbed a tea towel and began drying the dishes. She looked out the small kitchen window, pushed open to catch the warm evening breeze, and focused on the silhouette of the swaying grasses, charcoal gray against the black night sky.

"Good night then, Susie, and thanks for dinner." James's voice was gentle, as if he, too, hadn't been able to easily shed the mantle of memories that stirred feelings long repressed. She didn't turn around.

"Goodnight. Tom will see you out."

"Till tomorrow then."

"Yes, tomorrow."

Tom's chatter followed James outside and she watched them disappear over the dunes behind the back of the house, up onto the path to the winery. The path was unlit and it was dark tonight, no moon. But Tom knew it like the back of his hand.

She switched on the kettle and waited for Tom. Within minutes Tom had scampered back down the path and burst into the living room, his eyes bright and full of happiness. She handed him a mug of cocoa.

"James is so cool, Mum." She frowned at the sudden use of the word "mum". He tended to revert to it when he was feeling emotional. "How come you never told me about him before? He says you guys knew each other years ago."

"Oh, we were just friends."

"Best friends, he said."

"Yes well, times change."

"But you like him, don't you?"

"Drink your cocoa, it's way past bed time."

"But you do, don't you?"

"Yes, of course I do. How come you wanted him to come with us tomorrow?"

"Because I like him, too." He took a thoughtful sip of his cocoa. "And because he looked sad."

Sad? James? Now Tom had said that she realized he was right. She'd been so busy nursing her own anger and indignation that he should appear out of the blue and take over her life once more—and wondering what she could do to make him go before he could damage her hard-won independence—that she hadn't really looked at him, she hadn't really seen that look in his eyes, hadn't seen the sadness in the depth of his blue eyes.

Susie reached across the boat and took the hamper from Tom and secured it in the back of the boat.

"Morning!" James strolled out onto the jetty.

"Only just," replied Susie. "I'd have gone by now but Tom refused to go without you."

"Good one, Tom." He high-fived Tom.

She looked him up and down. "Left your city gear off then, today."

He looked down at his shorts and t-shirt. "Lucky Jorja found some of Pete's gear and lucky we're about the same size."

"Um." She looked him up and down, wondering why the same gear on Pete, despite his fit body, never had this effect on her. Then she noticed people had followed him with hampers. "What," she asked, "is all this?"

"Just a few essentials." He jumped down beside her and Tom in the boat. "I got to thinking about those cold sausage rolls and flat lemonade…"

"And you've bought hampers. Don't tell me. You had them delivered from the French Patisserie in town?"

"Well, I didn't make them up myself, that's for sure." He passed a bag of things to her. "And a few essentials for the night."

She peered inside. "An inflatable mattress? Good quality sleeping bag though." She nodded approvingly. "And…" He passed her another bundle. "A tent, Mac? Under the stars, remember."

"It might rain. You might be glad I brought it."

"Tom!" She shouted across. "Jump in. We'd better go while there's still room for us."

James inclined his head to hers as she untied the rope from its mooring. "I've got things to tempt you, too." The twinkle in those blue eyes caused her stomach to tighten with desire. "Later tonight. Maybe after a nightcap of flat lemonade, I'll let you have a little."

"Mac," she warned.

"It'll make your mouth water."

"I sincerely doubt that."

"Dark chocolate. The best."

In an effort to prevent him from noticing the smile that slipped from under her defenses, she turned away and stowed the rope into the bottom of the boat. By the time she turned around, James had taken control of the engine at the boat's rear. She sat behind Tom.

"You sure you want to steer? You never used to be so good with motorboats. Remember that time on the lake at home?"

He grinned as he applied the throttle and sliced through the calm water of the bay, out towards the gulf. "How could I forget? You saved me yet again. I've learned a bit since then. I keep my own boat on Tahoe so I know a bit about them."

"Who'd have thought it? James Mackenzie being practical."

"I'm far more practical than you know. Even to the point of needing to know exactly where it is we're going."

She smiled, relaxing under the strong sun and wind, and fresh salty air. "After ten minutes and two headlands, turn left."

Once out at sea, the wind picked up and they bounced

a little over the ruffled water. Tom laughed and stood up, still holding onto the side so he could feel the sea spray on his face. Susie knew that James was purposely aiming at the crest of a few waves to make sure Tom received a soaking. James didn't seem to mind that, in so doing, he was also soaking himself. He grinned at her, apparently not concerned that his usual immaculate look was less than immaculate. He simply slicked back his wet hair and it fell in the usual charming waves off his face, tanned and relaxed. If it weren't for me, Tom, and the shabbiness of the boat, Susie thought, anyone would think he was simply heading to Cannes for an evening with the rich and famous.

But he's not, she thought sadistically. He's going camping. And he'll hate it, with, or without, an airbed.

Susie swam a leisurely breaststroke back to shore, watching James and Tom play soccer as if they did it every weekend. It could have been like this, she thought bitterly, if it hadn't been for James's stupid behavior.

But it was no good, no matter what stray angry thoughts popped up, just seeing him play with Tom, unraveled them, combed out the knots that had been tight inside since he'd arrived. He moved with grace, as he always had, and he laughed easily with Tom. But Tom was always good company, she thought proudly. She ran from the shallows, laughing as Tom tried to defeat James with a bit of tricky footwork but he was no match for James who took command of the ball and sprinted towards the two t-shirts that represented the goal posts.

Susie's competitive instinct kicked in and she ran towards James, whose attention faltered, took the ball and slammed it down the beach into the opposing goal. She jumped up and punched the air. "Goal!"

"Yay! Mum!"

James took a few steps back and sat down abruptly, weakened by the sight of Susie's breasts rising out of her brief bikini as she jumped up and down with Tom. Her hair fanned up into the light, framing her. Her agile strength and understated beauty knocked the breath out of him. Game over. He'd been outmaneuvered all right.

She walked up to him, hands on hip. "Had enough?"

"For now, maybe. Ask me later."

She narrowed her gaze in suspicion. Keeping her eye on him she called to Tom. "Tom! Come on, let's eat."

They walked up to the line of pohutukawas that over-hung the beach, providing much-needed shade. James followed them with the hamper, watching them laugh and joke as they went. They had a closeness James couldn't help but envy. He hadn't had any time alone with Susie to ask her the question that was looming large in his mind. Was Tom his son? And it didn't look like he'd get any time alone on this trip. But part of him was happy. It meant that he could enjoy the day imagining that Tom *was* his son, imag-ining a life with both Tom and Susie that was worlds away from the one James had planned. Just the thought sent a thrill of desire and happiness through him that he never wanted to disappear.

He dropped the hamper on the ground and pulled out cushions and blankets first and tossed them to Susie. She shook her head in disbelief. "You and your comfort."

"Nothing wrong with comfort." He plucked a bottle of wine from the same hamper, poured a couple of glasses and a lemonade for Tom and then sat back and watched Susie distribute the cutlery and serviettes. Her hair fell in tumbling skeins, sprinkled with sand, to her shoulders. Her skin was perfect, unblemished and lightly tanned. And so was her figure, with its neat curves and long, lean limbs. The black bikini was utterly sexy, whether she thought so or not. Okay, it might not be as skimpy as he'd prefer, but it covered and showcased the shape of her breasts. He groaned and tried to think of something else. It didn't work so he dragged the second hamper in front of him. "Now, what would you like? Pate? Salmon? Salad?"

"Salad would be great."

"What kind of salad? Green, rice, chicken—"

"Mac!" Laughing, she reached over and took a selection of boxes from him and began spooning them onto the three plates.

"We've both earned a good feed, haven't we Tom?" Tom nodded as he munched on chicken leg. "It's harder work than the gym."

"More fun, though," added Tom.

"Heaps more fun." James exchanged grins with Tom and then turned to look at Susie and caught a wistful expression in her unguarded eyes that took his breath away.

She jumped up. "I'll go and get some water."

He watched as she disappeared into the bush.

"You like my mum, don't you?"

He looked around to see Tom watching him quietly. "Sure do. Not so sure she likes me much."

"Why? What did you do?"

How like a ten-year-old to cut straight to the heart of the matter. "I made a mistake."

"That doesn't sound so bad."

"It was a big mistake."

"Say 'sorry' then."

James nodded thoughtfully. It was true, he'd never actually apologized for his behavior. Years ago she'd disappeared off the map. He'd waited, expecting her to return, leaving messages wherever he thought she might be. But she hadn't returned to Glencoe and she hadn't returned his messages. And now? He'd somehow avoided saying the actual words.

"You know? You've got a good head on your shoulders. I'll give it a try."

"It'll work. Mum always forgives me when I mess up, so long as I admit to it and apologize."

"Thanks for the tip, mate." He jumped up. "Come on, let's go and see what she's up to."

They found her just inside the curtain of pohutukawas, drawing water from a pump.

"A pump? I thought this bay was uninhabited."

"It is now. But years ago?" She pushed aside a curtain of creepers. "Fantastic, isn't it?"

James couldn't see what she was looking at and preferred not to shift his own view. "Breathtaking," James murmured as he focused on her long, lean, limbs. With effort, he shifted his gaze from her chest to whatever it was that was holding her attention. He walked up beside her.

She shifted the veil of vegetation further to reveal a grand, two-storied, colonial house whose white paint had peeled, leaving scars of silvered wood, some rotten. Elsewhere, curling green tendrils of creepers probed into its nooks and crannies. "Been that way for over fifty years."

"Wow. Who'd have thought this was hiding behind these trees?" He looked up at the intricately balconied widow's walk along its upper story, set amidst a crescent of flowering pohutukawa trees. "It's like something out of a fairy tale."

Tom came running up behind them. "Perhaps there's a princess inside who needs a kiss to wake her up?"

Susie groped behind a ledge and produced a key. "Trust a person of the male species to believe a kiss could set everything right. When something's dead, it's dead."

James watched her walk up and take Tom's hand before opening the door. In that moment he realized just how much, and how deeply, he'd hurt her. And, for the first time, he wondered if he could ever put it right.

CHAPTER FIVE

James followed Susie and Tom inside. He was immediately struck by the smell of mice and dust. He ducked to avoid thick strands of gray cobwebs disturbed by the opening of the door. The two-story hallway was lit from above by a large, glass dome in the roof, from which a green-tinged light fell. Remarkably no panes had been broken and the interior was dry.

"It's Pete's family's old homestead. Apparently the family stopped living there in the 1950s when the road opened up from the town to Whisper Creek. It was too isolated here. It's only accessible by water now."

James rubbed his chin thoughtfully. "It's stunning."

"It's falling down." Tom suddenly appeared from one of the many rooms that led off the hexagonal hall. "Mum and I shelter here sometimes if the weather's bad."

"So why aren't we sleeping here tonight?"

"It's damp, and dusty. Definitely only a place for emergencies."

James's gaze shifted to Susie, who stood in the centre of the hall, the green light filtering down through the ivy that covered the glass ceiling, giving her an ethereal look. He had a jolt of déjà vu, as if he'd already seen her there before. *Ridiculous*. He turned away in confusion.

He opened the nearest door and walked in. It was heavy, good quality, and opened into a huge reception room on an incongruous scale, given its location, lit by large windows on two sides. He walked over to the windows, drawn by the view, dust rising with each step. He looked through French windows that opened out onto a wooden verandah. The blue of the bay was spread before him, just visible through the shifting leaves and branches.

Running footsteps approached and Tom slid up to him, arriving in a cloud of dust. James coughed and pushed open the warped windows with a shove. Tom made to go outside but James stopped him, placing his hands squarely on Tom's shoulders. "Careful. It's probably rotten."

James looked down at Tom and felt a surge of affection for the boy. Was he his? At the first opportunity he'd ask Susie. In the meantime he'd enjoy the possibility. But he knew, that whatever the answer he was Susie's boy, and he'd already developed a bond with him that would only grow.

"It's like a Rousseau painting."

"What?" Surprised, James looked out at where Tom was pointing at the thick vine and big green leaves.

"All jungly, dark and heavy and green."

"Yes, I guess it is. Do you like art?"

"Love it."

"Do you want to go to art school?"

For the first time Tom didn't answer his question directly but bit his lip and looked away. "I'll learn on my own. Art school's expensive."

James looked away also, feeling the boy's pain through

his too-adult words. "Yes, it is expensive. But if you want something, there's always a way."

Tom looked up at James with hope bright in his eyes. "Really? Do you *really* think I could do it?"

"Definitely." He squeezed Tom's shoulders and whispered in his ear. "Particularly if you have help from someone with a plan."

What was that feeling? That strange mixture of emotions that consumes you when you see two people—who you are, or *were*, close to—bond? Susie didn't know, but she couldn't tear her eyes away. She watched James dip his head to Tom and whisper something in his ear and her heart contracted at the expression on Tom's face as he looked up into James's —utter trust and hope.

She had to tell James the truth.

"This," James said as he walked towards her, "is perfect."

"Perfect, for what?"

"A luxury lodge. Nothing huge. We'd convert some of the bedrooms into en suites."

"You can't surely mean to convert this? Why would someone with heaps of money want to come here?"

"Because there's nothing else like it, it's picture perfect." He glanced out the window. "Or will be when it's finished. It's got the character that people coming from bland luxury will love."

She pressed her fingers into some rotting timber. "By character you mean rotting decay, I take it?"

"That's easy to fix."

"I don't know." She dug her finger nail in deeper. "It goes pretty deep."

"Nothing's unfixable, not if it's essentially sound." He caught her eye and then moved forward. "Just think, Susie." He paced around the room, looking up at the ornate ceiling, now covered in grime. "For access, you have the flat land above, perfect for a helicopter pad, and you're only half an hour boat ride away from any of Auckland's marinas."

"But that's not *good* access, surely?"

"It is for people with money who want privacy. I know people who'd rent this whole place out for their family for months at a time. And between times, it could be run as an exclusive lodge. It would have a professional kitchen and be a showcase for Whisper Creek wines.

"And you reckon it would be worth it? It wouldn't ruin this place?"

"Not if it's done right. Which it would be. You'll see when we go to Onihau next week. Guy runs something similar at his winery. You'd be able to develop the winery in line with your vision and invest in its operations.

She frowned up at him. "It'll require huge investment to get the place up to scratch. Where's the money going to come from?"

"Mackenzie Investments has been developing property for years. I've got the team. I'm assuming Pete would be interested in a joint venture, or selling it?"

She shrugged. "Probably, so long as he didn't have to be involved. His heart's in the Mackenzie country, even though he's kept hold of most of the original estate."

"Good. No problems then."

"For you, maybe not. But it would change the whole feel of the place."

"*Susie*, your and Tom's future would be secure. You'd both have the freedom to do as you like."

She was speechless at the sudden vision of a future where anything was possible. But, the door slammed closed on her vision. James still owned everything. He still had the power.

"It'll be fine," James continued, oblivious to the turmoil that was raging in her head. "I'll show you the kind of lodge I'm envisaging when we go to Onihau."

She nibbled her lip. "Just for one night, that's all I've agreed to. I need to be back for Tom. He's finishing school early next week."

"No you haven't, Susie," Tom piped up. "I'm staying in Auckland for the rest of the week so I can go to Matt's birthday party, remember. Aunty said it would be okay."

"That's settled then." James thrust his hands in his pockets and Susie could see his mind slipping into business mode as he looked around the place. "Next week in the Wairarapa we'll discuss the lodge and new equipment with Guy." He turned to Tom. "Does your mum have some posh clothes?"

"Yes." Tom grinned. "But she never wears them."

"Dust them off, Susie, you're wearing them next week. Lucia and Guy like to do things properly."

She tried to smile for Tom's sake. But still the seed of doubt nagged at her. Why was he doing this? Would this venture make her free, as he claimed, or tie her further to him? She and Tom followed James outside to where he stood looking up at the battered facade of the once grand old house.

"What a perfect place. I hope, one day, I'll find a home like this," said James.

"You must have a string of beautiful properties, all over the world probably."

"Properties, yes. A home, no."

She frowned. "You'll find a home one day, I'm sure you will."

His face held no trace of smile now. "Are you? I'm not."

"See!" Tom exclaimed proudly. "We don't need a tent." He tentatively rattled the collection of driftwood that he'd hammered into the sand behind where they'd be sleeping and James suitably admired it.

"The flag's especially good," James said, flicking the tattered white cloth marked with a skull and crossbones with his thumb and finger in lieu of any breeze. "Should ward off any pirates."

Tom looked at him with a pitying expression. "James, there *are* no pirates any more."

James laughed. "There *are* on foreign seas—Indonesia, Africa."

"But we're not near foreign seas, are we?"

Still laughing at his reduced status as an object of pity to a ten-year-old boy, James reached for a bottle of wine. "Where's your mother?"

Susie had made sure she was never alone with James. She obviously didn't want the conversation he wanted. But he *would* have it.

"She's just coming round the rocks." James followed where Tom was pointing. Susie was wearing a long sarong-type wrap skirt and a flowing shirt, both a soft orange. Slowly James stood up, transfixed as Tom darted over to her and took the basket of pine cones she'd been gathering from a neighboring bay.

Tom ran over and tipped them onto the pile of dry leaves and twigs they'd placed for the fire. James handed

Susie a glass of wine and she came and sat a little distance from James, leaving a space between them for Tom.

"It's a beautiful evening." James looked up at the sky, sipping his wine. "The stars are already beginning to appear."

"Do you know anything about the stars, James?" asked Tom as he flopped down beside James and pulled some blankets over him.

"No, sadly. I remember my brother, Callum, trying to teach me which stars were which, but I never paid much attention."

"You've got a brother? I wish I had a brother."

"Oh, you're better off without them. I have two—one in the South Island and one in Wellington. They argue with you when they're bored, they thump you when they're happy and they try to humiliate you as frequently as possible. It's one of their favorite pastimes."

"They sound mean. Don't they love you?"

James's heart melted a little at the boy's seriousness. Apart from the obvious need for a good education, he could see why Susie had decided he needed to mix more with other kids on the mainland. "Of course we love each other. We're just used to expressing it in different ways. Like, if you want to tell your mum you love her, I guess you go and say it, or hug her, do you?"

Tom nodded. "Yep. She likes that, don't you Mum?"

"Sure do." Susie's smile to her son brought a lump to James's throat. "Bread and cheese anyone?" She passed a slice topped with melting Camembert to James.

"Thank you. And, Tom, I'm sure she does." He glanced over at her. "Well, when *we* were your age, if Callum approved of something I'd done, he'd punch me in the arm, get my head in a head lock and slap me playfully on top of my head and say 'do it better next time.'" James shrugged. "That's love in our family."

"Wow!" Tom's eyes were large with surprise.

"Both my brothers are married now. Hopefully their wives have taught them that headlocks are not a good way to express love."

"I heard they'd got married." Susie, propped up on the multitude of cushions that James had insisted on bringing, pulled Tom closer into her embrace as she nibbled on the cheese and drank the wine. The soft warm breeze ruffled her hair and the flickering firelight gave her face a look at once familiar and exotic. "I can kind of imagine Callum married, because he got married young, didn't he? And his wife died. But Dallas? I was surprised. He always seemed like a confirmed bachelor."

"Not now. He's very happily married with two children. And Callum's wife, Gemma, had their first child six months ago."

Susie looked at him thoughtfully. "So you're on your own now—the only one unmarried, the only one without a family."

"Thank you, Susie, for pointing out how quite alone I am."

"Is that why you're here?"

Tom sat up and looked at them both in turn, his eyes suddenly bright with curiosity, obviously aware of some undercurrent of conversation. "Because James wants a family?" He turned to James. "Is it?"

James glanced uneasily at Tom. "You both think I'm lonely? No, I have a lot of friends, a whole other life in the US and big plans for the future. I'm just here to check on your mum. Your mum and I were friends years ago. I wanted to see how she was getting on. That's all. Make sure she was okay."

"Sure she's okay." Reassured, Tom dropped back down to the ground. Susie covered him in blankets. "She's got me to look after her."

James nodded. "So I can see. So..." He desperately needed to change the subject. "Coming back to these stars. What have we got?" He took a sip of his wine and drew closer to Tom and Susie. With Tom half-hidden by the blankets on the ground, James's face was close to Susie's.

Susie lifted up her arm and pointed to a cluster of stars already dipping towards the western horizon. He watched the pale underside of her arm and itched to stroke it. "That's Scorpius. Maori say it's the fish hook that the god Maui used to catch the Great Fish of Maui."

"The Great Fish of Maui is the North Island," Tom informed James.

"Is it indeed? That is some big fish," he added, distracted as he watched Susie shift her hand until her arm was nearly stretched across his body. "And do you know what that is?"

Tom yawned and James was too busy gently exhaling against her skin—watching her skin goose bump under the influence of his breath—to answer.

"It's the Sea Goat. Capricornus." She looked at them both. "Am I the only one who knows about stars round here?"

"I'm sure Tom does, but he's too sleepy. Besides we don't need to, with you here. You always were smart."

She withdrew her arm, suddenly self-conscious and pulled a blanket loosely over herself. "Not *so* smart."

He shifted onto his side, propped up by his hand. "Yes, smart."

"Not so smart now, though, am I? Trapped on a beach with you."

"And me, Mum!" Tom said sleepily before burying himself even further. His body stretched, pushing at them both, as he gave a great yawn. "I'm tired."

"Then snuggle down and I'll tell you about the stars."

Slowly the light faded until the only light was coming from the stars and their reflection on the sea. Susie recounted the stories about each of the constellations that were gradually becoming visible. James sat back, one arm hooked under his head, and listened to her stories, allowing her voice to wrap its way around him, to find its way into his heart.

Tom wriggled one last wriggle as his breathing deepened and he fell asleep.

James reached over and took hold of Susie's hand that was about to point out another star. "He's asleep." He lowered their joint hands until they rested gently on Tom. "Your hands are cold." He blew on her fingers and rubbed them between his own. "You should get under the covers. Keep warm."

Slowly she withdrew her hand from his, her eyes dropping to his mouth. He licked his lips as his thoughts refused to shift from her own lips. "Um." She shivered. "Guess you're right, Mac." There was something in her lowered tone, in the use of her nickname for him, that got to him. It was like a vibration that made its way deep inside of him, triggering a response of which he hoped she wasn't aware. She pulled the covers up until only her head was visible, and her eyes, which still held his gaze. "It's lucky..." She trailed off before clearing her throat. "...that you brought the extra thermal blankets. The night's colder than I thought it would be."

He felt an overpowering need to touch her, to feel the reality of her. Casually, he shifted his hand so he could touch her hair that spilled over the cushion. It felt like silk under his fingertips. She didn't move, didn't show she was aware of what he was doing. "It came with the rest of the stuff. Warm enough?"

She nodded, the slight movement betrayed by the gleam of the stars on her hair. "You?"

"Put it this way. You and Tom have all the extra blankets and I'm manly enough to cope with the cold, despite what you think."

She grinned and it warmed his heart. "Too manly to go searching for the sleeping bag or admit you might *be* cold, that's for sure."

"Absolutely. But I'm sufficiently in touch with my sensitive side to agree to share the blankets should the offer be made."

"It'll be made... When I've tired of watching you sit, uncomfortable and cold on the beach, I might let you share the blankets."

"So good of you. I promise to behave."

"How reassuring," she said archly. "And how unnecessary. In case it's escaped your notice, my son is lying between us both."

"*Your* son... Believe me, it hadn't escaped my notice. I'm fully aware of that fact. But, you know, I'd have behaved anyway."

"Right!" she scoffed. "*Mac*, your reputation precedes you."

"*Susie*, my reputation is exaggerated."

"Yeah, right. Lizzi was telling me the other month about how you disappeared with Dallas's nanny at Callum's wedding."

"Oh yes, I remember her. Nice girl. I spent a very chaste night listening to her life story."

"Yeah, right!"

"You don't believe me." He shrugged. "I don't blame you, but it happens to be true. It's hard to get rid of a reputation which one's worked so hard at acquiring. But if there's one thing about me that hasn't changed, it's that I never lie."

She didn't respond immediately. "No." Her voice had changed suddenly—it was so soft it seemed to float to him on the soft warm breeze. "No, you don't. Perhaps you *have* changed if you no longer need to seduce every woman you see."

James swirled the wine around his glass, trying to lessen the pain of her accusation by focusing his attention on how the firelight flickered, lightening the ruby red to flashes of orange. "Yeah. It was what I did for a long time. Like some people drink too much, some people become obsessed with sport, well, seduction was my sport." He turned ruefully to Susie. "A sport I was good at. But a sport that's lost its allure."

"You've *definitely* changed."

He turned away again and focused on the lazy roll of the waves on the shore. All he could see was the intermittent flare of white surf as it broke on the sand. Silence settled around them like a heavy blanket. The occasional call of a nocturnal bird and whisper of the wind in the flax were all that pierced it. Suddenly he felt the tentative touch of her hand on his. He didn't dare move because he didn't want her warmth to leave him.

"Or, rather, you've changed back to what you were like before. You're the boy I once knew, the boy I had some happy times with."

He licked his lips that were suddenly dry. She hadn't

forgotten about their time together, nor how happy they'd been. A happiness he'd taken for granted, a happiness he'd trashed, a happiness he had no right to now. "It's a wonder you can remember him. It was a long time ago." She withdrew her hand and he felt the chill of the air where her hand had been. He rubbed it, needing that warmth still.

"Not so long, really. Not if you've got a good memory." She looked up and caught his gaze in the darkening light. "Not if you don't want to forget."

An exquisite tension, pure and strong, gripped his heart. "And you don't?"

She looked away and smiled, a sad smile. "Some of it, maybe. But not all. Not the firelight, the jokes, the cold nights and hot days, the laughter..." She cleared her throat. "They're the times I like to remember."

"But not later?"

"No. Not later." Her words were cool and clipped and hurt all the more because of it.

The grip that had taken hold of his heart twisted a little. He looked up, above her, at the shifting silhouette of the leaves against the dark sky and cleared his throat. It was time to do what Tom had told him to do, what his conscience told him to do. "I'm sorry, Suse."

He didn't think she'd heard him at first because she didn't move. But then she reached out for his hand that he hadn't realized was tightly curled into a fist, and caressed it. "I know you are."

He frowned, examining her hand in his. "And how do you know this?"

"Because I *know* you, I know what you're like."

His smile faded. "You know what I'm like," he repeated, his gaze fixed on the stars that seemed to throb and pulse lighter with each passing second. "Then tell me, because *I* don't even know what I'm like any more."

"Oh, James." The unexpected note of tenderness in her voice nearly undid him, as did the use of his given name. Apart from when Tom or Pete were present, it was the first time since they'd met up again that she'd used it, instead of Mac. It seemed to denote a shift towards intimacy. "You were always kind. Always. I remember watching you with your brothers. Callum and Dallas would always be needling each other, competing, fighting. But *you*, you'd be looking around and you'd see me, watching you from the bushes. You defended me to your parents, talked them round, stuck up for me. Always."

He swallowed and licked his lips. "You were like a little puppy, all arms and legs and fierce eyes. You didn't care what anyone thought. Someone had to do the talking for you." He watched the shadows the darting flames of the fire cast on her face. "You were a funny wee thing. Haven't changed much either."

She threw a hunk of bread at him. "I may have been small but I wasn't funny. Anyway, we're talking about *you*, not me."

He picked up the bread and took a bite. "We've moved on to you." He had no choice but to move on to her if he was going to rid himself of the unwanted straitjacket of emotions that imprisoned him, which made him vulnerable. "Small and funny. What else? A great cook. I remember the cook-ups you'd do on the campfire."

"So I can cook—not that you're ever going to taste my cooking again until you display a little more of this legendary charm I keep hearing about."

"And you light up any room you're in."

She dropped her hands to her lap and fidgeted with her

nails. "Now *that* is a total exaggeration and I was just beginning to believe you."

He frowned. The light atmosphere had suddenly disappeared into the dark night. "I'm not exaggerating. Why would you think I am?"

"Because I'm plain and ordinary and definitely *don't* light up rooms."

"That's... that's rubbish." James could hardly get the words out. Why the hell was she saying such things? "You walk into a room and I can't keep my eyes off you."

"That's because you're *you*."

He shook his head. "You're kidding me, right? You *do* know how sexy you are, don't you?"

She spluttered and coughed as a crumb went down the wrong way. "James, please. You don't have to—"

"What? Tell you the truth? He rolled carefully onto his side, avoiding Tom who'd snuggled down lower and was sleeping peacefully. She lay on her back, the outline of her forehead, nose and lips just visible under the combined light of the stars and the fire. "I do have to tell you the truth because it seems you have no knowledge of it. Look at me." She glanced briefly and tried to look away but he caught her chin and lightly held her face so she had no choice but to look at him. "When I look at you the first thing I see are your eyes." He gently touched her brow, following its line around her eyes. She closed them and her long lashes tickled his finger. "I love two things about them."

She glanced at him from under lowered lashes. "Only two?"

He smiled. "But they're two big things."

"In that case..."

"First, they're beautiful. Your lashes are darker than your hair and... I don't know how it works but, although you don't wear makeup, your lashes form a line outlining your eyes, framing the hazel-green eyes like a portrait. A Mona-Lisa—except much prettier—watching me now, only me."

"I can see why you'd like that."

Desire tightened in his gut and lower. "But it's more than their shape and color. They see, *really* see things for what they are. No fooling those eyes. They see more than they should, perhaps."

Her hand came up to grasp his, held it for a moment and then dragged it off her face. "That's fanciful."

He sat back down but didn't take his eyes from hers. "No it's not. Your eyes affect me like no one else's. I can't hide when you look at me, I don't want to hide. Somehow... you release me."

They held each other's gaze for a long moment, during which the only sounds were the rustle of leaves on the land that rose steeply behind them and the soft sweep and drag of the waves on the sand. Then she shook her head. "I can't release you, James. Only you can do that."

The truth of her words hit him hard and he turned away as despair engulfed him. Could he never rid himself of the blank emptiness that filled him? An emptiness he was always trying to fill with women, with activity, with company, drink and travel. An emptiness that always returned.

Her hand reached out for his and he turned towards her. "You've lost your way, James. You knew it as a boy but, somehow, it's gone, you've lost it."

"Freefall, Suse."

"What?"

"I've been in freefall, nothing below me, nothing above me."

She pushed her fingers through his and closed her hand over and around his. "I have you now. Just for now."

And it felt so right. He could smell her perfume—not some packaged expensive fragrance, but the lemony scent of shampoo in her hair and the smell of fresh air on her skin. Just in that lungful of her, he felt absolved of guilt for the life he'd been leading. She was redemption to him. He couldn't mess it up. All he wanted to do was to turn to her and take her in his arms, to fill her with himself, to lose himself in her, mentally and physically, to come home to her. But he couldn't. Not just because Tom lay curled up at their feet, but because it was too soon.

He sighed and lay back, reveling in her warmth and tenderness. "Just for now," he repeated.

The words hung in the air, as Susie's breathing deepened and she drifted into sleep. He lay, his hand still in hers, and watched the imperceptible shift of the Milky Way overhead and listened to the lazy drag of the sea, which continued as if everything were normal, as if nothing had changed.

CHAPTER SIX

I t was cold when James awoke, his arms wrapped around Susie. Despite the discomfort, he'd not so slept soundly in years. They'd all snuggled closer together in the night but the slowly lightening sky was bringing a chill to the air. Within seconds of awakening, Tom had jumped out from under the blankets. Susie groaned and turned away, pulling the covers over her head.

"The tide's at its lowest now, I'm going looking for oysters. Coming?" Tom was pulling on his sweater and beanie against the chill.

"Later, Tom, later. Perhaps when the sun makes an appearance." He glanced at Susie who made no answer or sound. "Looks like your mum's not interested either."

"Pikers!" shouted Tom from over his shoulder as he ran towards the sea.

There was no answer from Susie. The covers had been pulled down from where Tom had leaped up. James shifted closer and pulled the cover over her shoulders. He lowered his head to hers. Even though she was fast asleep, she shivered. He shifted closer to warm her with his body and she snuggled back into him. He tried to think of something else, anything to keep his lust in check because it was that which had got him into trouble with Susie in the first place. He wasn't here to seduce her again. He was here to make amends before he left to start a new life. But his body refused to co-operate.

He looked across to Tom, who was happily peering into the gray rock-pools that the receding tide had exposed and then looked back at Susie. She frowned in her half asleep state and rubbed at her cheek where a strand of hair tickled. He shifted it off her face and the frown relaxed and her breathing deepened once more. He sighed, lay back and held her in his arms, never wanting that moment to end.

She woke up with a start and turned her face suddenly to his. He could still see the mist of dreams in her eyes. "James," she whispered.

He smiled. "Expecting someone else?"

"No. Where's Tom?" At that moment Tom scooped up something in the net and held it up to them. She waved. "Busy as usual. And you..." She turned to him. "I wasn't even expecting *you* to still be here."

Her smile was sweet and unguarded. He wanted to lift his finger and trace the upward curve of her lips but he didn't.

"Nowhere else to go, sweetheart." He might have been able to keep his hands in check but the endearment slipped out before he knew it. She frowned slightly. "Besides," he added quickly, wanting to see her relaxed smile once more. "I wouldn't get far on my own. I need you to navigate."

"So." She grinned. "I have power." She stretched out and he enjoyed the length of her arms and the rise of her breasts, so close to his body. She wriggled a little closer to him and looked into his eyes with a cheeky expression. "It feels good to have power."

He plucked a strand of hair and tucked it behind her ear. "Women always have the power. You just haven't realized it."

"Yeah, right. So powerful, the man always hogs all the bed clothes."

"That's because we're bigger and need more of them."

"Size isn't everything, you know." He grinned and she tutted in mock disapproval and poked him in the chest. "James! I know what you're thinking."

He grabbed her finger and held it tight. "Really? Then tell me."

She didn't try to move her finger, but held his gaze. He watched as the laughter morphed into something more intense, more sexual. He pushed his fingers through hers and brought her hand to his lips and kissed it. She shook her head but didn't say anything. He continued to hold her fist to his mouth, brushing his lips against her fingers. Then he moved away and released her, watching her fingers stretch out, pale and slight beside his own.

"James, I..."

"It's okay." He reached out with his other hand and stroked down her hair that was mussed at the side. "Unlike your hair." The tension dissipated, just as he wanted it to and she laughed, lost her balance and rolled towards him. In one movement his hand slipped around her body and brought her tight against him. He could see the precise moment when she felt how aroused he was. A shutter came down on her expression and she shifted away.

"Not much I can do about that, Suse. I have a beautiful woman in my arms."

She turned abruptly from him and sat with her back to him, pulling on her shoes. "It's automatic with you, isn't it?"

"Waking up in the morning wanting sex?" He sat up and began to reach over for her, wanting to touch her, to reassure her, but withdrew his hand before she noticed. "I can confidently predict that 99% of men are the same."

She glanced over her shoulder at him. "It wouldn't matter who you were with, then."

"Sex, maybe not so much. But making love?" He shook his head. "Making love's different. That's not automatic."

"Semantics. I'm not interested either way." She jumped up and peered out at the lightening beach, watching as Tom dragged the net to the far side of the bay. At that moment the sun began to rise up above the wide horizon, casting a ruffled red glow across the pale sea, illuminating the beach under its steady light. Birdsong filled the air.

He looked up at the shadowy trees above and stopped himself from replying to her with the truth. What good would it do her, or him, if he told her that she was the only one he wanted to make love to? He tried to smile reassuringly, as if nothing had changed. It had, but it made no difference.

"We should get going soon. Tom's got homework to do before he leaves for Auckland tonight."

"Tonight then, Suse. Dinner. Just you and me." He had a question to ask, a question she could only answer without Tom being present. And she knew it.

She didn't turn round but he saw the tension in her shoulders as she delayed her reply. Then she nodded. "Sure."

"Good. I'll pick you up at seven. Now... let's go and see what Tom's dug up for our breakfast. Last one there gets to eat it."

Susie had hardly said a word on the drive to the restaurant. She'd retreated from their earlier intimacy. That was okay, but he was going to find out what he needed to know, whether she wanted him to or not.

Even now, on the terrace of the exclusive restaurant, she'd rather look at the view—which he had to admit was amazing. The setting sun shed a soft raspberry glow through the low cloud that had settled over the Gulf. Center-stage was the volcanic island of Rangitoto, which sprawled across the Gulf like some sleeping giant. To the left, further still, were the lights of Auckland, topped by the Sky Tower.

He watched her as she checked out her surroundings with a professional eye—from the manicured lawns, clipped hedges and expensive, uplit artworks. She'd caught the sun at the beach. The flash of pink across her nose and cheeks, together with the green top she wore, made her eyes appear even brighter, even more striking than usual. She turned to him suddenly and it was his turn to look away.

"I haven't been here in ages."

"I like it."

She shot him a dark look. "I knew you would. It's smooth, sophisticated and so *not* what Whisper Creek is."

"It could be."

"James! It would lose its character."

"Okay. Let's leave it at that and we can talk it through with Guy. So... are you hungry?"

She took a sip of wine and shook her head. "I've already had a snack with Tom." She sighed.

"Sad to see him go?"

"Always. But it's for the best. I can't keep him here with me on the island. He loves his aunt and she adores him and he gets the best education I can afford and plenty of friends to play with." She smiled a quick brave smile. "It's for the best. It really is."

"I'm sure it is. Even if you *don't* really believe it. Anyway..." He pushed away the menu. He'd suddenly lost his appetite and topped up their glasses with wine instead. "Thanks for letting me tag along with you and Tom. I had a great time."

Susie smiled. "I know you did. So did Tom. He thought you were amazing. You've got yourself a fan there."

"And you? Did you enjoy it?"

She looked down at her drink. "You know I did."

He nodded. "Okay. Now, talk to me."

"You're very demanding. What do you want me to talk about?"

"Tell me about Tom. Tell me about his father."

"I'm surprised you took this long to ask me."

"Two things stopped me. Tom and..."

"And?"

"I didn't want to hear the wrong answer."

"Ah," she said on a quickly exhaled breath, as if shocked. "I wonder which answer you want to hear?"

He shrugged noncommittally. If he told her the truth now, she'd probably run a mile.

"I was married, you know," she continued.

James frowned and swirled his wine around the glass, studying it with an interest he didn't feel. "Yes, I know. Pete told me."

"Not many people knew. Just my family—mother, aunt and brother—we'd come up to Auckland by then. Lizzi—she knew I wouldn't want anyone from Glencoe to know."

"Meaning *me*."

"Meaning *you*."

"So, who was he?"

She sighed. "No one you knew. I met him in Auckland. We weren't together long. He died suddenly in a motor-cycle accident when Tom was two. Tom doesn't have any memory of him."

"I'm sorry. I..." He didn't know what to say. Hearing her talk of her husband made it all too real for him. "I had no idea."

"No, not many people did. I don't talk about it often."

"Too painful?"

"No. He was a good man in many ways. We just weren't suited. He was good with Tom, he loved Tom."

Loved him like his own? Or loved him because he was his own? "Tom told me when his birthday is."

"He told you that?"

"You must have got pregnant real soon after I last saw you." She didn't answer and James couldn't wait any longer. He needed to know. *Now.* He needed to know the truth, whether it would devastate him or not. "You didn't have that abortion, did you?" He wouldn't have believed it was possible to hear his heart beat so loudly above the pounding of the sea.

Her green-gray eyes appeared remote and grave. "Yes, I did." Her voice was so quiet, he thought he'd heard wrong. She must have seen his blank gaze. "Yes... I *did*," she repeated, louder this time.

The words slammed into his gut. She was lying. She had to be. "But... it all fits. Tom looks like me. He's the right age."

"I *had* that abortion, James. I had the abortion and then went straight out and got pregnant." If he felt pain at her words, he felt it doubly now, as her face twisted into a grimace that tried to hide a decade of grief. "I couldn't bear what I'd done." She drew in a deep breath. "Your parents wanted the abortion, my parents wanted it, and you... *you* wanted it. I was seventeen, too young to go against everyone in my whole world, everyone who I thought loved me. My parents wanted the best for me and thought an abortion was the best. Your mother wanted the best for *you* and considered an abortion was the best. Both of these I understood. But you? Who did you think it was best for?"

"I thought it was the best for both of us. But... I was young too."

"And now?"

"I was wrong. I should never have suggested it. I shouldn't have returned to university. I shouldn't have left you at Glencoe. I should have stayed."

"And done what exactly? Settled down to become a family man and farmer? Or taken me and the baby with you jet-setting around the world? A child wouldn't have fitted into your life. No, I didn't want an abortion. Everything inside me screamed against it, but I went ahead and had one because I was too young, too naïve, too weak to withstand the pressure. And I have to live with that decision every day of my life."

"And so do I." He turned away to hide the grief that the news had brought. She'd taken away any hope now that he'd ever have a son. Because she wasn't the only one who'd been affected by the abortion. He hadn't been able to prevent his hopes rising. Yes, he'd been shocked at first but that shock had turned into amazement and hope had blossomed. His future had suddenly seemed different to the one he'd envisaged. It was as if someone had lit a light at the end of a very dark tunnel, giving him a ray of hope. Susie had just extinguished that hope with one fell swoop. And all he felt was a deep well of emptiness and grief. "So do I, Suse," he repeated with a sigh.

He stood up and walked to the edge of the terrace, pushed his hands through his hair, and stared blankly at the distant lights of Auckland. He narrowed his eyes, focussing on the cluster of bright lights until his eyes watered.

James had only seen that he and Tom had shared the same coloring, the same build, the same sense of excitement and happiness he'd had as a boy, an excitement and happiness that had faded over time as he'd made wrong choices, been with wrong people, done the wrong things. But he'd not allowed his mind to notice the differences. The more serious nature, the solid sense of security and peace inside him, were things James had never had and never would have. All through their time together, he'd allowed his imagination to run riot and to think of all the things he could tell the boy, his son, to stop him from making the same mistakes he'd made. But the dreams had just shattered and disintegrated into dust. What a mess.

"I hadn't thought that you'd be disappointed Tom isn't yours." He turned to find Susie standing behind him, a confused frown on her face.

"No, I guess you wouldn't."

"You really hoped Tom was yours?"

"Yes." He drew in a deep, salty breath, once, twice, trying to draw back from the unwanted emotion, to find his usual superficial self, the charmer who always knew what to say. "Crazy isn't it?"

She didn't agree or disagree just looked out across the empty bay. "You don't have children from past relationships?"

He shook his head, not trusting himself to speak.

"I guess you made sure you didn't, after what happened to us."

He huffed a sad laugh. "I never had children and I never will have children."

"You can't say that. You don't know what the future will bring."

"I do on that score." He hesitated. Should he tell her that she wasn't the only person who'd done something rash? The only difference was that Susie had had a child and he'd made sure he could *never* have a child. No, there was no point.

He sighed and forced a smile on his face. "Would you like another drink?"

She shook her head. "I'm tired."

"Me too. Come on, we should go. We've an early start in the morning to catch the flight to Onihau." He reached out his hand to Susie, not knowing if she'd take it. But she did and they walked back up to the car, both silent, lost in their own private memories.

All the way home, Susie gazed out the window at the dark night, but her mind was focused on James, on the movements of his hands as he changed gears, and of the sadness she could feel emanating from him.

She had loved him. Then she'd hated him. Now? She couldn't afford to swing back to loving him again. *She couldn't*, she repeated fiercely to herself. He'd only turn tail and leave. He'd broken her heart once. She didn't even know if she had a heart to break any more and she wasn't going to test it.

But it had been so good last night, the sense of intimacy, with the three of them—and the two of them, she admitted.

And now, sensing his sadness and regret, the barriers she'd set around her heart had all but crumbled.

"How long do you intend to be here? With me? At the winery," she added quickly.

"Scared I'll outstay my welcome?" He smiled briefly. "Don't worry. I'm expected back in the States the middle of next week."

She bit her lip and nodded, turning away before her complicated feelings became too plain on her face. He was going. They'd only have a few more days together and then he'd be gone. That's what she'd wanted, wasn't it?

He pulled up outside her house and began to open the door. She reached out her hand to stop him. "No. Don't come."

"You sure? It's pretty dark out there."

"I'm sure. I've been taking myself home for a long time." Besides she was in more danger *with* him, than without him.

He nodded. "Okay."

Conflicting feelings surged through her. She rubbed one hand with the other, shaking her head. "Oh, Mac."

"What's wrong?"

She looked up at him then. "How about *everything*? You. Me. Here now. It's crazy. I don't know why you wanted to drag it all up again."

"Because I discovered where you were and I knew I couldn't get on with my plans until I'd sorted things out with you."

"Plans? What plans?"

"It's, er, a business merger of sorts."

"Really? Isn't everything—including the personal—always business with you?"

"Yes, it is. But why are you so angry?"

"Because..." She paused but couldn't think of anything to say other than the truth. "Because, I have to be. I'm trying to save myself because for years I hated you. I wanted nothing more than to see you rot in hell, along with the rest of your family and then you show up..." She bit her lip.

He reached out and took her hands in his. "Then what?"

"And I see you, *really* see you again and I don't know... The hate. It's gone. And I don't *want* it to be gone."

He closed his eyes briefly. "It was useful then, the hate?"

She shrugged off his hands and turned around. "Damned right it was. It gave me strength when I needed it."

He replaced his hands over hers and this time she didn't shrug them off. "You don't need it now though."

She shook her head and turned to face him, inching her face slowly towards him, hardly aware of what she was doing. She reached out and touched his arm. He took a sharp intake of air and closed his eyes.

"Don't, Susie." He didn't open his eyes and her hand didn't stop its caress, but moved onto his chest, her fingers spreading over his heart that beat out a rapid tattoo.

"I need to touch you, James. I *need* to."

Her hand shifted up from his chest and traced his lips. They were perfect. She felt the rush of his breath against her fingers and knew then, at that moment, that she needed more from him. Slowly she lifted her head until she was only inches from his face. Then she closed her eyes and pressed her lips to his.

Instinctively she shifted her body closer to his and moved her lips slowly, savoring every touch, every pressure and slide of her lips against his. He raised his hand and pressed his palm gently against her cheek, holding her to him as lightly, and yet as securely, as a fine gossamer thread. She felt the groan move up through his body as she opened her mouth and touched his tongue with hers.

With one movement he'd slid his arms around her and pulled her tight against him, responding to her kiss with a need that was as strong as her own.

The seconds of intensity could have escalated but she pulled away and he pressed his forehead to hers, his fingers in her hair, holding her firm, as they tried to calm their ragged breathing, tried to quiet the pounding of their hearts. Then he pulled away and looked at her.

"Suse, you're so beautiful." She heard the huskiness in his voice, the need that edged his words.

She shook her head, about to contradict him, but he raised his finger to her lips to still the words. She pulled away. "I'm sorry, I..."

"Don't be sorry." He cupped her cheek. "I'm not."

"I just don't want you to think there's more. A kiss is—"

"Just a kiss..." He smiled. "A good line. Should be in a song. But you're wrong. It wasn't just a kiss. It was something far more."

"And what of it? James, I can't risk letting you back in my life again. Don't you see? How can I trust that you won't get bored after a while? I can't risk it for me and certainly not for Tom. I can't do that."

His fingers tightened around her head. "You can."

"Think about it. My life is here, on this island. With Tom. You wouldn't be able to stand it for long. As soon as you began to feel trapped you'd be off. As soon as a pretty girl came by you'd be flirting."

"Do you really think I'm that superficial?"

"It's what *you* think that matters, isn't it?"

"Help me out here. I'm trying to turn my life around. I know what I want and that's *you*. Trust me."

"Trust you?"

He recoiled under her cold words, words designed to try to undo what her kiss had done. He withdrew from her immediately and sat back in his seat, looking straight ahead at the swaying grasses. "No. Of course you can't. It's too much to ask. Why should you?"

What had she done? "I must go."

"Sure."

He didn't make a move this time to walk her back to the cottage. She jumped out of the car and slammed the door. Before she'd set foot on her path, the car had roared off, leaving nothing but silence and self-recrimination.

CHAPTER SEVEN

Twenty-four hours later...

Susie's quick gaze swept around the aircraft. It was full of commuters. She pulled out her laptop and pushed her bag under the seat.

"You surprise me, Mac."

James turned to her, amused. "Good. I don't like women to be able to anticipate my every move."

"Usually I can, but this? A standard commuter flight to Wellington? Where's the charter jet, where's the helicopter? I didn't think the Mackenzies ever did anything normal like fly on scheduled flights."

"You were very clear about your expectations. No special treatment, you said. Normal business."

"I did. But I didn't expect you to listen, let alone agree."

"I don't agree, as it happens. Trouble was, there weren't any charters I could get hold of. Besides, it's good to see how the other half lives." He tried to stretch his long legs out but was constrained by the seat in front of him. "Even if it's only to remind myself why I never do it." He winced. "Is it always this crowded?"

"Yes, it is." She opened her laptop. "Now I suggest we talk about business. It'll take your mind off the fact that you're rubbing shoulders with the masses."

"So thoughtful."

"Okay." She opened a document. "As you know, we planted merlot, cabernet sauvignon, malbec and cabernet franc on the higher points of the site. Merlot plays to Waiheke's strengths but we need to continue to develop the cabernet sauvignon."

He didn't speak and she glanced at him. He was resting back in his seat, watching her. She sighed with irritation. How come this man, who she doubted had ever traveled on a scheduled flight before, could look so damn cool and comfortable?

"You're not concentrating, are you?"

He frowned, a small smile playing on his lips. "Yes, but not on what you're saying."

"Mac!"

"I can't help it. You're looking very beautiful this morning. I like that shirt." He smoothed his forefinger down the length of her arm. "What is it? Some kind of silk?"

She shook her head. "I don't know. I doubt it. The local mall doesn't usually sell silk."

"Ah." He nodded. "That's why I didn't recognize it." He smiled guilelessly and sat back in his seat.

"You were right." Susie couldn't help but grin when she saw him focus rapidly. "Ah, that got your attention, didn't it?"

"Of course. I'm always interested to know when someone believes me to be in the right. I'm right about so many things, what is it you're referring to?"

"We need to improve our catering facilities."

"Yes, we do. Guy can help with that. He could also help with importing grapes from Marlborough to increase the variety and quantity, if we think that's the way to go. Although I'm not so sure."

"Me neither. New machinery, yes. Improved catering, yes. But let's keep the wine-making to those grapes we grow on the island. We can do well using only our own." Susie clicked open a spreadsheet. "You see, I've got the production schedules and projections for the next few years here. This column shows the volume of grapes we anticipate harvesting this season and this one the production, if and only if we import grapes to supplement the harvest." She froze, his finger was once again on her sleeve.

"You shouldn't shop there."

"What?" She glared up at him.

"Not at the mall. I'll get my assistant to send you some stuff from Hong Kong. She's got a great supplier."

She let her head fall back against the seat. "You're really not interested in this, are you?"

"Oh, I'm interested all right."

A tingle of heat started where she didn't want it to start and she automatically swiveled the air vent down on her heated face. "No, you're not. You won't listen to any of these facts and figures about wine."

"I'm not one of you crazy multi-taskers. I focus on one thing at a time. That way"—his fingers smoothed down her forearm—"I can concentrate all my energies into one thing and do that one thing extremely well."

"And that one thing would be?"

"You, of course."

She shook her head. "No, Mac. I've told you. Last night, it... it was mistake. I can't be— I'm not interested."

"I don't believe you." His finger lifted to her chin and turned her face towards his. "Your eyes are soft and dark, your lips, parted. See, you've just licked them."

"I have not," she said indignantly, even though she realized she'd responded exactly as he'd described. She could smell his subtle yet sexy aftershave, get lost in those dark eyes where humor and complete and utter charm were present in equal measure. He seemed so sure of himself, and so sure he knew her. And he was right but she'd be damned if she'd let him know it.

He dipped his head to her. "You smell so beautiful. What is it?"

"Shampoo." She shot him a quick glance. "From the supermarket," she added for good effect. "Store brand."

He gestured with both hands. "You see? What other woman could make supermarket rubbish smell divine?"

"You, Mac, see what you want to see, smell what you want to smell, do exactly what the hell you like. Aargh!" She retrieved her earphones from the pocket of her computer bag and put them in. "I'm going to reply to some emails if you're not going to listen to me. You'll just have to amuse yourself."

She tugged down her skirt that had somehow worked its way up her legs by the open glances that James was giving them.

"Don't worry, I will."

She read and reread a line of email, the words floating before her eyes without meaning. Her head full of the unwanted stimulus of his aftershave, the way his trousers tightened over his thigh, nestling too close to hers for comfort—she could feel its heat searing her stockinged leg—and his words, flirting with the air hostess who assured him that nothing, absolutely nothing, was going to be too much trouble for her.

Frustration and, yes, she couldn't help but admit it, a massive dose of lust, simmered inside her. Her body responded to him, just as it had the night before, just as it had ten years ago in the hayloft. She closed her eyes as she relived that night of sheer pleasure and lust with James. It had been her first time and he'd been as tender and as loving as she knew him to be. So that, despite the discomfort, the one thing she remembered was absolute pleasure and absolute joy at her connection with him.

"Susie." James tickled the back of her hand with his finger. "The nice lady's asking you a question."

She opened her eyes, trying to repress the residual sense of arousal that still filled her. She looked up to see the puzzled glance of the stewardess. "Tea or coffee, ma'am?"

"Neither thanks."

The stewardess smiled, a wary smile, and passed James a coffee. Susie noticed it wasn't one of the usual coffees out of the pot. She'd somehow produced an espresso for James. Of course she had.

He plucked an earphone from her ear and whispered into her ear, his warmth breath caressing her skin. "You should chill more, you know, Susie."

"That's all very well for you to say. You're rich and have no worries. Any money I've made has been swallowed up with... living expenses." She'd nearly referred to Tom and she really didn't want to discuss him with James.

"You don't have to worry about money any more."

"Why does that make me feel like a kept woman?"

"I don't know. Perhaps it's some subconscious wish coming through?"

She sighed and shook her head. "Just promise me one

thing. Over the next few days, don't confuse me with one of your women. I'm *me*. Don't flirt with me. Don't turn on the charm. It won't work." She narrowed her eyes as the silence only grew.

"I'm promising nothing," James eventually murmured. He took a sip of his coffee and flipped open a newspaper.

"Promise me," she repeated.

"Baby, I never make promises I can't keep."

She dropped her head on the back of the seat and closed her eyes. Standing on a cliff top, with nothing but vast emptiness all around, was nothing compared to this for danger.

The helicopter circled once before landing on the helipad at Onihau Estate.

"I might have known the public transport wouldn't last."

"I think once was more than enough. Although," he said as he waved to a tall man waiting for them, "it *was* interesting, fun even, talking to real people."

"No fun if you do it all the time."

"Now *there*, Suse, is the difference between us. You don't like people and I do. You're threatened by people."

"And you're threatened by loneliness."

Rather than the irritation she'd expected, James pressed his lips together in a rueful smile. "We know each other so well."

The engine stopped and James slid open the door for Susie to exit. He followed her outside into the dry heat of central Wairarapa.

"Guy, I'd like you to meet Susie Henderson. Susie is an

old friend and manager of Whisper Creek Wines on Waiheke Island, the winery I was telling you about."

"Pleased to meet you, Susie. And this is Lucia." He indicated a beautiful woman walking down the path towards them. Her exotic looks suggested both mediterranean and Chinese ancestry.

Susie shook hands with them both, feeling instantly shy with these two glamorous people. Three glamorous people, she thought, glancing at James.

"Lovely to meet you, Susie." She and Lucia fell into step in front of James and Guy as they walked through the Mediterranean-inspired formal gardens. "James tells us you're originally from Glencoe."

"Yes, my family had been there for generations. They were shepherds at Glencoe and my father had an interest in developing the viticulture there."

"Must have been wonderful growing up with all that open space."

"It *was* wonderful." Susie glanced up at James who was obviously listening.

"Susie and I used to hang out together when I was home from boarding school." He grinned. "Terrorized the neighborhood."

"Do you miss it, Susie?"

"Yes, and no. Dad got me interested in growing grapes early on so it was a natural progression to work in a winery. It was always his dream to run one."

"And did he?"

"No. He died the year I left Glencoe. But he'd have loved Whisper Creek. I know he would."

They stopped outside some open French windows and Lucia gestured for her to enter the house. It was a huge room, with high ceilings, light and airy with windows on three sides, filled with simple, but obviously expensive, furniture.

"I'm sure he would. And if anyone can help you with the winery, Guy can. He grew up on his family vineyard and knows everything there is to know about running one."

Lucia turned to James. "And, James, you're looking well. But you always do. The rest of your family's arriving early evening. It'll give you a chance to have your business meeting with Guy and then relax with them tomorrow."

Susie's heart sank. *The Mackenzies? Here?* It was bad enough being with James, but the rest of them? There were nothing but bad memories associated with their family and Glencoe.

"Are the kids coming?"

"Just Gemma and Callum's baby. Dallas's two are being doted on in Wellington by a cluster of great aunts. You'll be staying here for a few days, won't you?"

James exchanged looks with Susie. "Unfortunately, not. We have to get back." He chucked Lucia's chin. "Don't pout, it's childish."

Guy clapped his hand on James's shoulder and smiled across to Susie. "Anyhow, let's get on with business, shall we? Sooner we start, the sooner we can move on to sampling some of it."

"I'll bring some coffee."

Susie and James followed Guy through to a book-laden library, minus a desk and chairs, but complete with stone-colored soft suede sofas and a round table.

"So, Susie. I've heard of your winery, of course. And watched your progress in a few short years. You guys have done well to avoid the effects of last year's heatwave."

Susie could relax once more. She was on familiar territory.

. . .

After a couple of hours they walked out onto the terrace, having looked around Onihau Lodge and worked out what new equipment Whisper Creek should invest in.

"Would you like to try some?" Guy asked as he showed Susie the bottle of wine they'd been talking about.

"Sure." As they tasted and chatted, she didn't hear a car approach the front of the property. Suddenly there were shouts and laughter and James looked up with a grin as his brothers and their wives emerged from the house. Susie shrank away. It had been a long time since she'd seen them and she wasn't looking forward to it, aware of the bad memories that would come flooding back.

"Susie! Good to see you. It's been years." Callum's grin was warm and welcoming.

Susie stepped forward. "Yes, it's ten years since I was last at Glencoe."

"You should come down, we've made a few changes but things are pretty much the same. I remember you always had an interest in the land."

"Like my father did." She couldn't resist a reminder to the Mackenzies that her father had died on *their* land, in *their* employ. Only she knew his death had been caused because he'd been forced to leave the land he'd grown up in and loved, because of her. He'd been distraught, and she doubted she'd ever get over the guilt.

"That was a tragic accident," Callum said. "We made sure it could never happen again by fencing off the gully." He looked up as a pretty, petite redhead walked towards them, carrying a sleeping baby. "Meet Gemma." Callum pulled the smiling woman into his arms, with a gentle brush of the soft downy head of the baby.

"Lovely to meet you, Susie," Gemma said. "I hear you knew this lot, back in the day."

"Kind of. From afar really. Except for James." James and her eyes met and connected. She looked back at Gemma. "He was nearer my age than Callum and Dallas. I would have been nothing but an annoying kid to them."

"You were to me, too, Susie." James laughed. "I didn't mean it." He backtracked as he received one of her best glares. "You remember Dallas?"

"Of course." Susie instantly felt shy. Dallas had always seemed so grown up when she was small; he'd carried the weight of the family's fortunes on his shoulders for years. Strangely, he appeared younger now than when she'd known him. She extended her hand, which Dallas ignored, giving her a brief hug. He drew back and smiled at her.

"You're all grown up, Susie Shaw."

"I should hope so." She felt embarrassed by his close scrutiny. "I must have been around ten when you left Glencoe."

"Cassandra," called Dallas to a tall, dark-haired woman emerging from the house. "Come and meet James's friend, Susie."

Cassandra took Susie's extended hand. "Pleased to meet you, Susie." Lucia joined them as the others drifted away around James as they caught up with each other's news.

"I hope you'll be able to stay for a few days? Lucia said you might be leaving in the morning."

"Well, James has to return to the States and I've work on Waiheke. So..." She looked across to where James and his brothers were talking and laughing. Her gaze lingered on James. He looked so natural there, in the company of men for a change, just like the man she used to know. Then he turned and his eyes met hers. He smiled and she found herself smiling back. He walked over to her.

Cassandra followed Susie's gaze and watched James approach. Cassandra's lips twitched as she looked from one to the other. "James." He kissed her on the cheek. "I was just asking Susie how long you're staying."

His eyes hadn't left Susie's. "We both have commitments tomorrow, I'm afraid. It's just a flying visit."

"Shame. Next time, you must stay longer," said Lucia. "Come on, Susie, I'll show you to your room in case you'd like to rest or freshen up before dinner."

They walked past where the men were grouped, now joined by James who immediately made some comment which had them all laughing. How did he do that? Within minutes have men and women charmed and entertained? She sighed and followed Lucia through the double doors, almost walking into her when she stopped suddenly at the first door along the wide hallway.

"Here's your and James's room."

As luck *wouldn't* have it, everyone stopped talking right at that moment. The doors to the living room, where everyone was gathered, were wide open and Susie knew they'd heard Lucia.

Susie shook her head, not wanting to speak. She could feel a heavy blush rising through her body. "Me and James?" She glanced through the open doors; everyone was looking at her expectantly, including James, a smile playing on his lips as he watched, entertained, as to how she was going to respond. She dipped her head to Lucia, trying to make her words private. "We're not a couple, Lucia. We're old friends and business colleagues now, but we're not, you know..." She shook her head in embarrassment.

"I'm so sorry." Lucia looked appalled. "Come on, I'll

show you another room." She continued down the corridor. "It's just that James, he's so, well, you know..."

"Yes, I know. He has a reputation for..."

"Exactly..."

"But...we're not..."

"Sure." Lucia said too quickly. She looked back at Susie. "Sorry."

"No problem," Susie mumbled. But, as she followed Lucia down the hall to a spare bedroom, Susie knew she'd lied. There was a problem. A big problem.

James watched Susie and Lucia disappear inside and tried to swallow the grin that threatened to spread over his face. He turned to his brothers and Guy and his grin faded. Everyone was staring at him.

"What?" He asked accusingly.

"You're not *with* Susie?" Callum asked.

"Of course I'm *with* her, I'm just not..."

Three men shook their heads, with the same puzzled look on their faces, and stared right back at James.

"What?" asked Guy. "Not... what?"

James shrugged. "I'm not *sleeping* with Susie."

Three pairs of eyebrows shot up into foreheads in identical amazement.

"What is *wrong* with you people? Haven't you heard of platonic relationships before? Haven't you heard of a woman and a man being together and yet not having carnal knowledge of each other?"

"Heard of it," said Callum with characteristic abruptness, "but not in relation to you."

James didn't contradict Callum. What was the point when he spoke the truth? "Well, there's always a first time."

"You *are* kidding, right?" Dallas managed to say.

"No, I'm *not* kidding."

"Who *are* you and what have you done with my kid brother?"

James groaned. "Give me a break."

"No way. This is far too entertaining."

"Hey, if not for me, don't give Susie a hard time."

"You *do* like her, don't you?"

"Of course I like her. I'm investing money with her, we're, well, old friends."

"You've got history, haven't you?" Dallas asked suspiciously.

"'History?'" asked James, stalling. "Why don't you say 'previous' and be done with it? You make it sound like a conviction."

"I'm beginning to wonder."

"Well don't."

"Hey, guys, stop bickering, will you?" Cassandra joined them and intervened. "It's lovely to meet a friend of yours, James. Susie's wonderful."

James couldn't help softening. "Yes, she is." He immediately regretted it when he heard Callum's exclamation. He turned to Callum. "For once and for all, Susie and I are *not* a couple. I'm investing in her business, she just happens to be an old friend, but we're *not* sleeping together."

"It must be serious then." Callum swigged back his beer and placed the bottle, which looked too small in his large hands, on to the table.

As usual, Callum had hit the nail on the head without any preliminaries or frills. It *was* damned serious. His brothers knew it, his sisters-in-law knew it, his friends knew it, and he bloody well knew it. Why didn't Susie know it?

James sighed, accepted another glass of wine, and

watched his family shift focus and talk about their children. Even though they were here as something of a break, they couldn't stop talking about them. He caught Lucia's uneasy gaze and they exchanged embarrassed smiles. His family sometimes forgot that Lucia was having difficulty conceiving and was increasingly finding it hard to cope with talk about children.

He indicated with his head that Lucia and he should move away.

"How are you, Lucia?" He slipped an arm around her and drew her to him and kissed her on the cheek. He didn't let it drop until he felt her relax in his arms.

"I'm fine," she said too quickly. "But I'm more interested in Susie. She's lovely. Too nice for you," Lucia teased. It was exactly his thoughts and he couldn't find his usual banter to counter her words. Lucia looked at him with a surprised smile on her face. "What? No riposte? No come back?"

"No. You're absolutely right. She *is* nice. Too nice for me."

"Self doubts, James? That doesn't sound like you."

He couldn't find any energy, any way in which he could dredge up the old James. "Maybe not, but it *is* me. I'm good at hiding them."

She raised her eyebrows in surprise as she patted the seat beside her for him to join her. "I had no idea. When did this start?"

"Always. I have two big and powerful brothers, a domineering mother who adored me, and a father who I'm far more like than Dallas, except no one can see it. Except Susie."

Lucia nodded. "She's your Achilles Heel. She knows you like no one else."

"She knows me and she hates me."

"I doubt that. I've seen the way she looks at you."

James turned to look at Lucia. "Really? Which way?"

"Like she's concerned for you, worried about you, looking at you like you're definitely more than a business partner. James, she cares for you."

He shook his head. "You've got it wrong. She's putting up with me because she has to. Her partner wanted out of the business, which is her whole life, and I'm the only one who wants in. She needs my money."

"I think there's more to it than that."

He shrugged. "If there is, then she's hiding it well."

"She mentioned her son to me earlier, I guess she doesn't want to rush into anything because of him." She paused. "Have you met him?"

"Yes. He's a great kid." He looked at Lucia, suddenly realizing what lay behind the quiet question. He slipped his arm around her shoulders. "Guy said you're still waiting on the results of the latest IVF. It'll happen."

He felt her sigh and shake her head against his shoulder. "I don't know if I can take much more. Each time, I'm so hopeful, so full of expectation that... it's just so much harder when it comes to nothing."

"Don't give up."

"That's all right for you to say, James. You'll marry when you find the right girl and have a tonne of children."

"No. That won't happen. Anyway, this is *you* we're talking about. *You* and Guy and it *will* happen, I know it."

Lucia laughed and pulled away. "Even though I know you're talking me up, I feel better. You can always do that, James. It's your gift to the world."

"Sure." He turned back to the window to watch Susie walk away from the group, into the house.

"Why don't you go and find Susie. I think she's a bit embarrassed by my *faux pas*. I'm really sorry."

"Doesn't worry me. But then your mistake is completely understandable."

Lucia looked into his eyes and kept her hand on his arm, detaining him. "Is Callum right? Is this for real?"

James felt the tension of emotion ball up inside him, making him unable to speak for a few moments. He cleared his throat and still found he couldn't speak. He pressed his lips together in a rueful expression and nodded and looked away.

She smiled. "Tread carefully, then. Susie doesn't look the sort of woman to forgive things lightly."

"You're right there. But, then, she's had it rough."

"Go find her."

He walked past the room that they were both to have shared and hesitated by the spare room. He knocked on the door. Susie answered it straight away, as if she'd been waiting on the other side. She still hadn't changed for dinner, but had obviously been standing by the open windows that looked out to the rolling hills planted with grapevines. Her low-heeled pumps had been kicked off and her bag sat, still packed, on the bed.

She looked lost and, unusually for her, anxious. James fisted his fingers in restraint. He desperately wanted to take her in his arms and hold her, to make everything all right. More than that, he wanted to take those damned corporate clothes off her. Best of all he'd have preferred to see her naked. Second best, at least in clothes that she felt comfortable in—shorts, t-shirt, casual clothes that suited her outdoors, practical nature.

"You okay?"

She nodded, too quickly. "Sure."

"Lucia's mortified she had the wrong idea."

Susie shrugged. "It's not her fault."

"You mean it's mine."

She sighed. "Look, James, I'm sure you didn't tell her we were a couple but I'm equally sure she's not used to providing separate rooms for you and your... friends."

"True. Come on, get changed. Dinner will be soon." He took hold of her hands and looked deep into her eyes. "What is it?"

"It's just weird, being with all your family again. I mean, my family were their employees and I still feel like one."

"You don't feel like one to me. You never did."

"That's because you're you."

"So I'm not so bad, then."

"I didn't say that."

"What did you say?"

"You've always been able to see me for who I am."

He nodded. "I know."

"How?"

"Because it was the same for me. And you knowing that, Susie, is what made what happened all the more difficult for me to understand."

"What?"

"You believing that I slept with you on a dare."

"Because you did."

"No, I didn't. I was young, I'd drunk too much and the guys were having me on. All it did was to make me look at you in a different way. All it did was make me go up to you and instead of sharing a joke, to take your hand and ask you to dance. All it did was to make me drop the screen that lay between you and me and make me see you for who you really were."

He still hadn't looked her straight in the eyes. Instead he watched her throat constrict as she swallowed hard.

"A girl, you mean?"

"More than that. A girl who was beautiful, a girl who somehow, completed me." He nodded and stepped away.

"Completed you? What does that mean?"

"I don't know. It's what I felt. Correction, it's what I still feel." He walked backwards away from her before he pushed his luck too far. He wanted to go on, wanted to tell her what was still in his heart but was scared it would drive her away.

"If you felt like that, why didn't you come to see me?"

"Susie! I did, you know I did. You refused to see *me*!"

"That was after I'd had the abortion, after I'd discovered you already had a girlfriend, after Dad had died and your mother had tossed me, my mother and my brother out of the shepherd's cottage that went with his job and off the estate. After my life was in tatters."

"And you blamed me."

"Of course I did."

"Do you still?"

"Partly. But I blame myself more. I should never have listened to my parents or to you. And..."

He lifted her chin gently with his finger. "And?"

"I should never have believed your friends over you."

"It's past. We can only move on from here."

"But how?"

"Step by step. Slowly. I don't want to make the same mistakes again." He moved forward and kissed her forehead. "Come on, let's go." He grinned. "Otherwise all those protestations I've been making about our relationship being platonic won't be believed."

She sighed and shook her head. "I'll get changed."

"Don't worry about what to wear. Just wear your usual..." He indicated her clothes with his hand as if unable to express it.

"Usual chain-store rubbish?"

"I didn't say, 'rubbish'. No." He shrugged. "I mean... whatever you wear you look beautiful in."

She shook her head but smiled. "James," she said reproachfully.

"What?" he asked, indignation playing on his features. "I mean it."

"I know you do." She walked up to him and kissed him quickly and softly on the lips. "I know you do," she repeated more softly. "And that's what makes you so very special."

Susie walked towards her suitcase and James backed out of the door, confused, swept away by the soft kiss and her words. He closed it behind him and leaned back against it, unable to move towards the light and laughter that spilled out from the open door at the end of the hallway. He felt as if he'd been given an electric shock. His heart pounded and he felt more alive than he had for years. He'd wanted absolution and he doubted he'd ever get that. But Susie had just given him something far more valuable. She'd shown him a future that wasn't bleak, a future that held a light of hope. And he wanted that light. He wanted her.

CHAPTER EIGHT

James sat back and watched his friends and family relax. The conversation flowed and the teasing and laughter was easy, showing the rapport the group had together, a result of years of friendship. Usually James was the center of attention, always a part of the action, but not tonight. Tonight, he sat back and watched his family and friends talk. Tonight, his mind and heart were full of the woman whose absence he felt more acutely now than he had over the last ten years. Crazy, he thought to himself.

He shifted his gaze away from the group to the dark swimming pool upon which pinpricks of light danced, reflections from the outside lights. He focused on the bright shimmering spots, his eyes prickling with their brilliance. Crazy, he repeated, to think seeing her again, helping her out financially, would make things easier for them both. It had made things a whole lot more complicated. He'd planned a future based on the assumption that there would be no love, no family for him. But now the world had shifted from under his feet and he'd have to return to the States and cancel those plans. It wouldn't be a problem because his personal life and his business life had slowly merged into one until they'd become indistinguishable. And business could always be canceled.

"You're quiet."

He turned to find Cassandra had removed herself and had sat down beside him. She was one person from whom he couldn't hide his thoughts. "Yeah." He smiled. "Happens once every decade or so."

She raised an eyebrow. "Laugh it off all you want, but you can't fool me."

"Cassandra, I didn't think anyone could fool you, not for one moment, especially not my big brother. He's far too direct and honest to fool anyone."

"And so are you, behind the charm."

He felt his façade slip away, along with his smile. He sighed and pushed his fingers through his hair. "What the hell am I going to do?"

She sat back and took a sip of her wine, apparently unsurprised by the question. "Tell me about her."

"How did you know it was about Susie? And not some other woman, some other deal, some other—"

"Just a random guess." She grinned.

He paused, trying desperately to make sense of the myriad thoughts and feelings that ran chaotically through his mind and body—surging, retreating, swamping him with confusion. "I've known so many women, I've lived life all over the world, doing what I wanted, *where* I wanted, with *whom* I wanted. Non-stop excitement. But..."

"It's not enough?"

He shook his head. "No." He could hardly say the word but he could feel it, like a bitter pill stuck to his lips that he was trying not to swallow. "No," he repeated even more softly, shaking his head.

"Then stop that life and start a new one. Sometimes it takes a bit of time to work out what you want."

"Ah, but you see, I think I've always known what I wanted. Trouble is I messed up, I'm not good enough for her."

"Come on, that's not true. Give yourself more credit than that."

He shook his head. "You don't know what I did."

"Whatever it was, it couldn't have been that bad. I'm sure she must have forgiven you by now."

"I don't think..." The words died on his lips as he turned to follow the gaze of the others. Susie stood there, looking hesitant and... sensational.

"Go to her, James, and make it work. You deserve it."

Did he? He couldn't agree but he had no choice but to rise and walk over to her. He was drawn to her at some instinctive level that he couldn't understand. And he didn't want or need to understand. He held out his hand to her and she took it. He curled his fingers around hers and gripped them like he was never going to let them go.

As soon as James took her hand, Susie forgot about being self-conscious in the dress that clung to her every curve. She'd packed the dress on a last-minute whim. She'd worn it only once before, not liking the way men had stared at her in it. She hadn't analyzed her impulse to wear it again, but now, seeing the way James was looking at her, she knew that that was why she'd brought it. Deep down, she wanted James to stare at her in the same way. But she hadn't antici-pated the others being here and she felt self-conscious. But the secure warmth of James's hand wrapped around hers, made her nerves disappear.

He drew her hand to his lips and kissed it. "You look beautiful," he murmured. And, for once, she felt it.

"Hey, Susie!" Gemma called. "Come and sit over here."

As they walked hand in hand over to the others, a part of Susie—the no nonsense, cool-headed woman who didn't like to reveal her emotions in public—thought she should release his hand, but she couldn't. He had a hold on her in more ways than just his hand. For some reason he was able to find the chinks in her armor and connect with emotions she didn't even know she still had. She had a frightening feeling that there was no going back, no covering up the girl who was revealed simply by James's presence. Under the soft lights of the terrace, their relationship had just moved to a deeper level. She didn't know where it would lead, she only knew she'd need all her strength if she was going to stop it from taking over her life.

She drew in a deep breath and tore her gaze from James whose soft smile and hungry eyes were both admiring and devouring at the same time. She forced herself to look at Gemma who glanced between them with a smile.

"Tell us about yourself," Gemma said. "We don't often get to meet James's friends."

"The interrogation has begun," James said. "Sorry, Susie. There's no getting away from it. I'll get you a drink."

As James walked away, Susie sat down beside Gemma and Lucia, trying hard to work out how she could recount a past that didn't show the Mackenzies in a bad light. "Nothing much to tell. I live a quiet life on Waiheke Island. My son visits at weekends and I work hard at the winery pretty much 24/7. The owner wanted out of the business and so James has bought it. He's interested in building up The Lodge business. Hence our visit here."

"Great idea," Lucia said. "Guy says it's remarkably

successful and if anyone has enough contacts with people to make a lodge work on Waiheke, it'll be James." Lucia hesitated and then leaned towards Susie. "Tell me, how did you go from rural Mackenzie country into growing wine on Waiheke?"

Susie looked uncomfortably at James who passed her a large glass of wine. "The long way round. Hard work, long hours and sacrifices."

"Sounds so unlike you, James." Dallas laughed.

"Hey, wait a minute. I work smart."

"And are you saying I don't?" Susie asked.

"No, of course I'm not." James's voice changed when he addressed her. "You've done what you have to do." He turned to the others. "Susie's worked her way from nothing to where she is today. A solo mum with a kid, it must have been hard."

Susie pressed her trembling lips together tightly as she listened to James proudly list her achievements.

"Very impressive, Susie," Dallas said, leaning back, watching her consideringly. "That takes a lot of dedication."

She shrugged. "I had no choice. I had to look after myself and my son. And luckily I shared the same vision for the winery as its previous owner."

"And now you've got James. What vision for the winery do you have, James?"

"Susie and I are in agreement," James said quietly, looking at her. "Invest in some new machinery, create a high-end lodge, but otherwise, keep the wine as it is. It's excellent. There's no need to change it."

"Did you consider amalgamating with a larger winery, say one of the Marlborough vineyards, import their grapes, increase variety and quantity. It could push Whisper Creek into a different league."

"We considered it." James glanced at Susie. "But Susie prefers to be independent and, in this case, I think it works."

"Right." Dallas looked from Susie back to James and back to Susie again. "There's a lot to be said for independence."

"It's the way it has to be." Susie looked at James. It was a message for him and only him. No matter how he looked at her, no matter how he made her feel, she had to look after herself, she couldn't let him threaten her hard-won independence. Not when he could destroy it again, on a whim. "It's the way it has to be, James."

He turned away abruptly.

"So..." said Cassandra, obviously picking up on the change in atmosphere. "If you're not staying on at Waiheke, James, where to next?"

"We're both returning to Auckland tomorrow. Susie's off to Waiheke and I'm leaving for the States. I have"—James's gaze faltered slightly—"I *had* things planned that I need to change. Then, well, we'll see." His gaze didn't shift from Susie's, but she tried to avoid it, focusing on sipping her wine. "You know me," he continued, "never still for long."

"Certainly never home for long," Dallas said.

"Apart from that time, James, when you came back to Glencoe," said Callum. "I never did understand what that was all about."

James shifted his glance and frowned at Callum. "I needed some time out after my first year at university."

"It lasted a whole year! A year in which you did nothing but hang around, getting in everyone's way."

Susie looked quizzically at Callum. "That doesn't sound like James."

"Well." Callum looked at James. "Crap happens sometimes that gets to you. Even if you're James."

"Were you depressed?" Susie asked directly.

James didn't meet anyone's gaze just raised his eyebrows in surprise, as he swirled the wine around his glass. Slowly he lifted his glass until it was level with her face and subtly shifted his gaze from the glass to her eyes. She was shocked by its dark intensity. "Who me? How likely is that?" His words were designed for humor but his glance, that only Susie could see, wasn't. The others laughed. Susie didn't. And nor did Callum.

"Pretty likely after what Dad did to you," Callum said.

Dallas ground his teeth and looked away. "I should have been there."

"You couldn't be everywhere," Callum said. "Besides, I sorted it. James and I sorted it."

"What happened?" asked Susie.

"Just Dad being a bastard as usual. He liked to use his sons as punching bags. James had avoided most of it because mother sent him away to school. But when he returned he copped it worse than either of us. He wasn't used to it, like I was," Callum added. "Didn't know the signs."

"You should have told him," Dallas said angrily.

"I tried. I told him to leave but he wouldn't and I wasn't always around to stop it. God knows what James was hanging around for—he just kept saying he was waiting for someone."

Susie bit her lip and looked down. Had he been waiting for her to return?

James casually hooked an elbow over the chair behind him and turned away to talk to Cassandra. Everything he did, Susie suddenly realized, was done with an air of control and ease, done with the need to hide. He'd hidden the fact that he'd been depressed from just about everyone, including his own family. What else had he been hiding? Did he truly regret what had passed between them all those years ago? And, if he did, what difference did it make to her now? She'd created a life for her and for Tom. Was she going to just sit back and allow it all to be taken away from her now?

Then she made a mistake. As the conversation drifted on to other subjects, James looked at her and didn't look away. She tried to breathe normally, she tried, *really tried*, to tear her eyes away from that hot, melting gaze, but her heart raced and her body reacted as if his hands were caressing her skin, as if his lips were on hers. How the hell was she going to keep her distance from him? She *knew* there was no long-term place for James in her life, she *knew* she simply couldn't risk her and Tom's livelihoods. And she also knew it was too late to risk her heart. They might not have tomorrow, but they had tonight.

"Fancy a walk?"

Susie shivered in anticipation at James's whispered words, nodded and rose out of her chair. Dinner had seemed interminable despite the great company and wonderful food. Because with every passing moment, the tension within her twisted and tightened until she could hardly sit still in her chair, aware as she was of every move-ment, of every word James uttered. He'd been seated oppo-site her and their heated gaze had clashed with increasing frequency and intensity as the night continued, until the need to be alone with him had become overwhelming.

He opened the door and she stepped outside and inhaled the fragrant, still warm, air. There was no sound of civilization to shatter the peace, only the occasional eerie call of an owl and the rustle of the leaves of the stately lime trees that lined the drive. "It's so beautiful here. And quiet."

"You're used to the ever-present sound of the sea, I guess," said James putting his arm around her. "Come on, let's explore."

They walked in silence around the pool, through a small gate, and crunched their way down shell paths that were bright under the solar lights that hung above them in the gently swaying trees. They stopped at the edge of the trees where the view opened out to a field of vines.

James turned Susie within his arms. His dark hair and clothes blended into the dark trees and sky behind him but she could see his face and eyes, and she could see his expression—hungry and restrained at the same time. The breath left her body as if she'd been winded and she inhaled the warm night air, willing for calm, willing herself not to be drawn into him and devoured by him, not to lose herself in him.

But her will dissolved as soon as his fingers splayed out around her hips and lower, and pulled her tight up against him. She didn't pull away. His hands and body warmed hers with a heat she suddenly desperately wanted. She slipped her hands around his back—molding her palms to the contours of his body beneath the thin shirt—and breathed in his masculine scent. She brushed his collar to one side with her lips to inhale him more deeply. The movement of his hands over her body sent delicious sensations skittering erratically through her body. She shivered.

"Cold?" He whispered against her hair.

"Yes. No." She sighed, shaking her head, bewildered. "I have no idea."

He laughed and pulled her closer to him. She nestled

her head against his chest and his arms wrapped around her until she could feel every part of his body, hot against hers.

"Were you waiting for me, James? At Glencoe. After you left university?"

"Of course. I couldn't find you and I knew how much you loved Glencoe. You'd always said your future was there. So I waited for you. But you never came."

The thought of him waiting, and her not knowing, devastated her. She turned her face against his chest and groaned, her hands moving onto his body, around the smooth texture of his shirt until they met at his back. "I didn't know." She looked up to him, and they were so close, breathing in each other's scent, each other's breath. He cupped her face and drew it tenderly closer to his. "Oh, James," she whispered. "What a mess. What a waste." Her heart ached for what might have been. Their eyes locked. All she could see was the need, *her* need, reflected in his eyes, lit by the twinkling lights in the trees overhead.

"I've missed you, Susie."

He didn't move but she stretched up and touched his lips with her own. "And I've missed you," she whispered. Suddenly his mouth was upon hers, claiming it with a kiss that swept away the remnants of her doubts and transported her into a place she hadn't dared dream about for ten long years.

Everything around them receded into some distant place that held no significance beside the exquisite tenderness of his lips on hers. It was all she could feel, all she could taste and all her body needed, brought together in that one kiss. His tongue barely swept her own, his lips were soft. There was no taking in the kiss, only giving. Slowly he pulled away and brought her hands up to his lips. He kissed the tips of her fingers in turn and then kept them pressed against his lips as he looked into her eyes.

"I *need* you, Susie."

She knew exactly what he meant because she felt it too. This wasn't a time for words of love, for words of promises, for...words at all. There was only an essential need. And *that,* they both shared.

He put his hand protectively around her shoulders and they began to walk away from where the family were congregated to the back of the house, to where the French windows of Susie's bedroom could clearly be seen, open and welcoming.

"James!" Cassandra's voice floated out across the still night air.

James winced. "It's Cassandra. You go on and I'll go and say goodnight to everyone. I'll join you in a moment."

He kissed her lightly on the lips and shook his head as if he couldn't believe what was happening. She watched him disappear inside the high vaulted living room, whose windows were open onto the balmy night, before stepping inside her room.

CHAPTER NINE

Susie leaned against the window jamb, willing the slight breeze to cool her heated skin as she listened to the distant conversation, her ears discerning James's low voice and thrilling to the sound.

She tried to focus, tried to think clearly, tried to make herself move, to stop what was about to happen. But she couldn't. All she could do was remember the heat of his lips pressed to hers and how good it felt. How *right* it felt. She raised her hand and touched her lips with her fingertips. Then she heard the prolonged noises of people shouting goodnight and doors banging. Then footsteps. She turned away from the window and watched the door.

There was a quiet knock. She walked over and opened it. James stood there. No bottle of wine, no social prop to act as an excuse for being there. She took hold of his hand and pulled him inside.

She pushed the door closed and slid her hands around his body, pressing her cheek against his chest. "James," she whispered. She held herself tight against him, relishing the strength of his body against hers, his lips pressed against her hair.

Then he lifted her chin with his finger so their eyes met. "Are you sure about this?"

She swallowed and nodded. "For now. Yes. Only for now. I can't give anything more. I can't risk anything more."

His arms slid around her body and their lips found each other's with a searing urgency that only ten years of separation could bring. As their lips, mouths and tongues tried to erase the years, Susie slid her hands under his shirt. Her fingers were tentative to begin with but, at the feel of his bare flesh, prickling with goose bumps despite the heat, her fingers pressed into his skin, easing over his muscle and sinew, wanting desperately to know all of him. But before her hands were satisfied, he suddenly pulled away.

His gaze swept her body appreciatively. "Suse." He shook his head. "Look at you. You are *so* beautiful."

"Come on, I've hardly got model looks." She felt uncomfortably reminded that James was used to the company of glamorous women.

He kissed her fiercely before standing back, stroking her cheekbones with his thumb, frowning. "You, Mrs. Henderson, are delusional. He nuzzled her neck and inhaled her scent. "You drive me crazy. I can see I'm going to have to show you how beautiful you are, if you can't see it yourself." Lazily, he looked her up and down, his hooded eyes revealing every indecent thought that entered his mind. Then he caught her gaze once more. "Where, I wonder, shall we begin?"

His finger trailed down her neck, under her dress, and hooked her bra strap. He continued to follow the line of her strap, dragging his finger against her skin, sending a rush of sensations deep inside her. He stopped when he reached her bra. He swept his thumb over the swell of her breasts as they rose and fell far too quickly. Then he looked up under lowered lids. "Here?"

She licked her lips and nodded.

He dipped his thumbs under the sheer lace of her bra and she caught her breath. She clamped his hand against her chest. "James!"

He smiled, a sweet, soft smile and kissed away her exclamation. "I've waited ten years for this, I'm going to savor every moment."

She leaned in to him and kissed him, such a long, slow kiss that he was left in no doubt as to what she wanted and how quickly she wanted it. But it made no difference. James was in control. As he caressed her tongue, his hands moved slowly around her back, ratcheting up the tension inside her. She moaned and eased her hips against his, needing to feel his power and strength. She felt him smile against her lips as he lifted her up and laid her on the bed.

He stepped away and she sat up.

"Suse... lay down."

"But—"

"I said I was going to take this slowly, show you how beautiful you are and I will. Even if it means I have to tell you what to do."

"Tell me." She hardly recognized her own husky tones.

"Lay down."

She did as she was told. He came and sat on the edge of the bed, his hand briefly caressing her foot before trailing it up her leg with frustrating slowness, smoothing his thumb and index finger along her shin bone up, over her knee, until his fingers spread out around her thigh. She caught her breath as his fingers caressed the inside of her thigh. She shifted so he could reach where she wanted him to reach. His hand immediately pulled away.

"Suse," he said warningly. "Move back to where you were."

She was impatient for him, but she shifted.

"That's better. I said slowly, Suse. And slow it will be. We've waited a long time for this. You can wait a little longer."

"You go," she said before inhaling sharply as his fingers found their target, "as slow as you like."

As the light began to creep in through the open windows, Susie shifted from under James's embrace to see him better. He was fast asleep. He looked so young when he was asleep. Serious. And sweet. That was her James.

Her James.

She swung her legs to the floor and pulled on her robe. She tied the sash and walked to the open window, suddenly needing to breathe. She felt enclosed, claustrophobic. She stepped onto the private terrace and clutched the rail. Fear. That was it. He'd driven through her defenses and she was scared she'd disintegrate and let go of the tight hold she had on the world. She'd given him the power. She needed to keep the power.

She closed her eyes as she heard him approach her.

"Morning, beautiful." He nuzzled her neck.

She shouldn't, she knew she shouldn't, but she leaned back into his embrace. His hands slipped around her body, one sliding under the fine fabric of her gown, and embraced her. Whenever he was close to her, her fears dissolved into the ether.

"How come you smell so divine? How come you *always* smell so divine?"

"Soap."

She felt his laughter against her neck. "Don't tell me," he murmured, his breath causing her skin to peak in goose bumps, sending shivers of excitement coursing through her body. "Supermarket brand."

"Exactly." She twisted in his arms, placing her hands on his shoulders, meaning to push him away, as she struggled with her need to retain control. But, instead, his lips found hers and she melted into his kiss. His hands slipped down to her bottom and he pulled her to him and she could feel his arousal pressed hard against her body.

She had to move away. "James... I—"

But her words were stopped by a placement of his finger against her lips. "Susie. Give me some credit. I know what you're thinking."

"How can you?"

"I spent my days with you as a kid, watching you as you reacted to the world, marveling at your courage and strength. I know what makes you tick."

She shook her head. "I've changed."

"No." He brushed her lips with his own. "Not so much."

"A lot of time's passed since then."

"Time in which I've thought of you, of what you did, wondering what you're doing, thinking about you..." He sighed. "I know you're scared. You're probably planning the fastest way you can get back to Waiheke, back to Tom, back to your life."

She looked at him, amazed.

"I see I've surprised you. But you're easy to read, so straight up, so straightforward. You've worked hard to gain your independence, to be not as vulnerable as your parents were to others. And it's worked. And you're not going to lose that now."

"It's scary, James, trusting someone again, giving myself to someone again. We're so different, you and I, from different worlds. What if you leave me again, maybe not now, but at some point in the future? I don't know if I can handle that risk. I mean"—she shrugged—"what do I really know about you and your life in the States?"

He stopped stroking her head and she noticed a slight frown appear between his eyes. Then he started stroking her head again. "That world is irrelevant to us."

"But it's your world."

"*Was* my world. I can't go back to it, not now. What I want is here."

She swallowed as she let his words sink in. She waited for the panic to begin but there was none. She looked at him. "Here? In New Zealand?"

He grinned and reached for her hands. "Here, with you, Susie. It's you I want."

She looked up at him incredulous. "Truly?"

"Yes, truly."

She grinned as joy bubbled up inside her. But with the joy came tears. He lifted her chin and brushed away the tears from her cheeks.

"I hope that those tears are ones of emotion rather than sadness?"

She nodded. "James... I, you're all I want too. I trust you."

He nodded, his grin spreading wide across his face, his eyes shining. "Good, good. We'll go back to Waiheke and make a life for ourselves." He closed his eyes and frowned, turning away. "But I have to go to the US tomorrow, I have... business to tie up."

She slipped her arms around his waist and leaned her cheek against his back as he reached for his phone. "I don't want you to go."

He slid around, putting his arm around her, even as he rang a number. "And I don't want to go but I have to."

She looked up at him brightly. "I know! I'll come too. Tom will be more than happy to stay at my aunt's for a few more days and play with his mates and we're not busy at the winery until next month. How about it?"

James frowned. "I'll be busy. There's the winery's annual winter party I've organized. Other things I have to attend to."

"Party? Sounds good fun."

He hesitated only a moment—a long moment in which she was beginning to wonder whether he really did want her—before he nodded. "Okay, Suse. A few days there to sort out business and then back to Waiheke. For both of us."

"Both of us." She sighed as she sank back into his arms, against his lips and his body as he tossed the phone on the table and rolled back onto the bed.

CHAPTER TEN

Twenty-four hours later, Napa Valley, California

"We're nearly here, baby."

Susie felt the softest of touches on her cheek and turned and kissed James's finger. She stretched and looked out the window at the moving countryside, softly blanketed by a mist through which the bare branches of tall birch trees rose like giant feathers dividing fields of gnarled vines. But it was neither of these that made her gasp. The entire ground was carpeted with the brightest yellow flowers.

"Mustard blossoms. They always surprise people. It's not what you imagine in winter."

"Nor is the fog, to be honest, but it's all beautiful."

"Looks like the fog will burn off soon. We get a lot of clear blue skies in winter too. We also have great food, great red wines, roaring fires, hot pools... and when we've tired of that, there's bed."

Susie sighed. "Bed... Yes, I like the sound of it all, but especially bed." She turned to face him, tracing her finger down his shoulder, his arm, to his hand, firm on the steering wheel. She followed the undulations of his knuckles and shook her head in disbelief at the shivers of need that her touch inspired. "But not to sleep."

She was rewarded with a deep intake of breath from James. The muscle in his jaw flickered as he tried to rein in his desire. Just seeing how she affected him fueled her own desire. He put his foot down hard and they roared up the road. She closed her eyes and smiled to herself.

James swung the Porsche around the circular drive with a flourish. He reached over and kissed her. "Wakey, wakey, sleeping beauty."

"I'm awake all right," she murmured against his lips, as she slipped her hand around his head and brought him closer to her. She felt him groan against her mouth, as their kiss deepened. His hand moved up the bare skin of her legs, under her skirt. She clamped his hand so it couldn't move. "Unless you want me here and now, I suggest you stop." She grinned at the look of frustration on his face.

He sighed and nuzzled her neck. "Susie, you have no idea what you do to me."

"Oh"—she opened the door—"Yes, I have."

He slammed the door shut and walked up to her, putting his arm around her, drawing her close. She snuggled into his body, still amazed that she was here, with him. With him... she repeated to herself.

"Then perhaps you'll describe it to me. I'd like to hear you tell me what effect you have on me."

"You want me to talk dirty?"

Just then the concierge walked out to meet them. James kissed her chastely on the top of her head. "Later," he murmured before greeting the concierge.

Susie looked up at the soaring cream limestone columns and arched portico. "Wow. This is grand."

James took her hand and they followed the concierge and porter into the marble interior of the winery. "The previous owner had it designed to be a modern take on a classical Italian winery. It won all the architectural awards when it and the hotel were built five years ago. Come on, you can get settled, enjoy a mud bath if you like."

"A mud bath? You're joking. I wear my gumboots to protect me from mud. I don't want to roll around in the stuff. Not without you, anyway," she whispered in his ear. Her words had the effect she wanted. She could feel it in the grip of his hand as it tightened around hers and in the way he plucked the key from the desktop and quickened his pace.

When they reached a wide flight of steps, they began to run, up the stairs and across the mezzanine to one of the half a dozen doors that led off it.

Laughing, they burst into the suite, flung down their carry bags and she jumped into his arms, her legs curling around his hips, his hands skimming around her bottom, as he walked over to the bed.

They fell onto it, their limbs entwined, their laughter turning to moans, and the moans to gasps.

It wasn't until much later that they lay in a tight embrace, trying to regain their breath. Susie's heart was full and, acting on pure impulse she kissed him and looked into his eyes. "I love you, Mac."

And she could see he felt the same way. But then, she saw something else. His eyes clouded as if a sudden thought had cast a shadow over his feelings and he withdrew and rolled onto his back, but only for a moment. Then he swung his legs onto the ground, stood up, and readjusted his clothing. He turned back to her and gave her a brief smile. "I need to go out, Suse. I won't be long. I have something I need to take care of."

"What is it? Shall I come?"

"For just about everything else but this. Just one meeting, I promise and then we'll sort out business, go to the winery's annual winter party, and have a few days vacation before we return home."

"Home," she repeated, not even trying to stop the stupid grin from spreading over her face. "Home, I like that word. It's different now."

"Because I'm in it." He grinned before turning to pick up jacket.

She kneeled on the bed and slipped her arms around him, resting her head on his back. "For once, your robust ego is correct—because *you're* in it."

He turned and kissed her on the cheek. "You have no idea what it means to me either. A home with the woman I love and my son."

"Your son?"

"Susie, it doesn't matter to me if Tom isn't my biological son, he'll be my son from now on. I love him, and I love you."

He turned and Susie put her head to one side questioningly. "Sounds like you love Tom more? Should I be jealous?"

He stood up and walked over to the window, pushing it open, letting the cool winter air inside.

"James, what is it?"

He didn't speak immediately. "It's just something I have to deal with. I'll tell you all about it later."

"Is it something I should be worried about?"

"No." He turned to her with a quick, tense smile. "Nothing. Have a spa—mud or no mud. Look around the winery. I'll have someone come up and show you around. I'll only be gone a few hours and when I return"—he approached her and put his hands around her waist—"I want you dressed in your finest so I can show you off."

She shook her head, smiling. "Show me off? You're one mad man. Just as well I love you."

He pressed his lips together as if trying to suppress something but there was no smile. He kissed her quickly on the lips. She wondered if it was what she'd said. The words had just slipped out somehow. She'd always been like that. She'd suppressed her feelings for so long, there didn't seem any stopping them now they'd been released. "Have I said something you didn't want to hear?"

"No, my darling, you didn't. It's just that... I can't concentrate just yet." He pushed his fingers through his hair and shot her a brief smile. "Later." He kissed her once more and then grabbed his coat and was gone.

She stepped onto the balcony and shivered, watching his Porsche turn around and return the way they'd come. She had no idea where he was going. So... he had a secret. She shivered again, but it wasn't through cold this time.

Only a few hours later the cars began arriving, disgorging the rich and beautiful, dressed in their finest. Susie didn't move. She continued to watch until she saw James's car amongst them. He was alone and jumped out and tossed his keys to the attendant who drove it away. He was with her in minutes. She stayed by the window. He entered the room and turned on the light.

"Susie! I thought you'd have already gone down. You look beautiful. I love the Grecian one-shouldered look." She looked down at the dress she'd selected because it was the cheapest in the boutique adjoining the winery.

"You didn't tell me it would all be so expensive."

He frowned. "You don't have to worry about money any more. I have an account. I told you to put it on it."

"I'm not doing that. I have some pride, you know."

He sighed and walked over to her, all sign of his earlier strain forgotten. His hands rubbed her cold shoulders while he searched her face. "You, Susie Henderson, are one stubborn person. Anyway, what are you doing here all alone in the dark? Did you have a good afternoon? Did you enjoy the winery tour?"

She shook her head. "I didn't go." She bit her lip. She didn't want to say that she couldn't face the tour, not while she was wondering what he was doing, not while she was wondering if she'd just make the biggest mistake of her life. Or the second biggest. "Not in the mood. Anyway..." She turned away in his arms and picked up her bag. "How was your afternoon? Get your mysterious meeting out of the way?"

"Susie. I'll tell you all about it. I promise."

"How about now?"

He shook his head. "Not now. I can't. It's too soon. I can't risk..."

"What can't you risk, Mac?"

He sucked in a breath, which made her even more nervous. "Suse, just leave it. You've got to trust me on this one. We're late. I need to change and get down there."

. . .

They walked under the massive Palladian arch, supported on either side by marble statues of naked men, their hands reaching up behind them as if to support the arch. Clusters of marble grapes dangled from the central point of the arch.

"What do you think?" James asked.

Susie's flat sandals made no noise on the marble floor, unlike the high heels of the other women, the shouts and noise of conversation that echoed around the massive, echoing marble space, built to impress. Only it didn't work on Susie. "Think? It's"—she shrugged—"amazing." And it was. Beautiful people moved everywhere, fitting into the grandiose design of the building and its furnishings. "And it's a million miles away from Whisper Creek."

"Over eight thousand to be exact." James grinned. He took a couple of glasses of champagne from the tray of one of the many dinner-suited waiters and handed her a glass. "To us?"

She raised her glass. "What's happened, James? This afternoon you were tense, nervous about something, but now you're happy."

He put a possessive arm around her. "Sure am. I'm with you, aren't I?" He looked around. "Now let me introduce you to a few people." He acknowledged a wave from a group of people who descended on them, effectively stopping any further conversation between the two of them.

With each passing hour, Susie felt more and more unhappy but she couldn't figure out why exactly. Yes, the winery dwarfed Whisper Creek in every respect, from the scale and quality of the building, its operations and the wines, to the clientele, who wouldn't even have heard of little old Waiheke Island, let alone have been there. And then there were the people. At least here in the cellars where they'd progressed to, the differences between her world and this one, were less obvious. With the light shining down from the far end of the brick vaulted cellar, it appeared never-ending. She jumped as she felt James's hand on her waist. She leaned in against him with a smile. "I can't believe you're interested in Whisper Creek when you own something like this."

"Used to own."

Susie frowned and turned to face him. He was standing with his back to the overhead light and she couldn't see his expression, but she could hear the tension in his voice, a tension that had been present ever since they'd landed in the US.

"But, upstairs, the chairman talked about you as if you owned it."

"I did. I've just arranged to sell it."

"But I don't understand. What's going on?"

"It's complicated. I should have told you in New Zealand. It's just that I never, ever expected you and I would..."

"Become lovers again?"

"Yes. The most I hoped for was to see your future settled and to have some kind of forgiveness from you."

"That's all you wanted? You didn't want a relationship with me?" Susie felt a sickening feeling slip low into her gut. The residual flavor of wine soured on her tongue.

"I didn't dare *dream* of a relationship with you. I thought my life was about making the best of a bad job. So I made other plans."

She frowned. "What plans?"

At that moment a group of men and women walked up and exchanged hearty greetings with James. She knew him.

He'd always loved people and parties and he'd made a life here for himself in the US where he was on everyone's guest list, on good terms with everyone.

Susie just didn't fit in. For the first time that evening, James had actually released his hold of her waist. He was busy talking with an animated group, laughing over jokes she didn't understand and didn't want to listen to. Susie crossed her arms awkwardly and slipped back. She had nothing in common with any of these people. She stepped away, but James turned and looked for her and walked over to her.

"Not much longer. I've done my bit, the speeches are over, five minutes and then I'll take you upstairs and ravish you."

She grinned, despite herself. "Is that right?"

He tried to pull her closer. "Absolutely. Do you want to know what I'm going to do to you up there?" He looked around and pulled her into the shadow of a huge oak barrel. He nuzzled against her neck.

She giggled. "Mac." She tried to bat him away. "Not here, someone may see."

"I don't care."

He pulled her tight against him. Despite herself she felt her body react. She opened her mouth under his and their tongues tangled in an increasing frenzy of arousal that made her forget about the long hours she'd stood talking to people she didn't want to know and God willing, would never see again. Too soon they pulled apart, panting, their foreheads pressed against each other's.

"I'd have you here, now, if I could."

"Do what you have to do with the others, go, say good-night and then come to me James. I'll be waiting upstairs."

She smiled as she watched him hesitate, take a deep

breath and smooth back his hair and join the group of people. She slipped away from the party, away from the bright lights through into the relative quiet of the lounge bar. There, she paused. Ten minutes for James probably meant half an hour and she was thirsty.

She walked over to the bar, empty except for an elegant woman who leaned against an open window, smoking. She was dressed in a tight white dress, which accentuated her tan and her amazing figure. She turned to watch Susie as Susie ordered a pot of tea to be taken to her room. She glanced at the woman, struck by her feline green eyes, accentuated by her short dark bob. The woman smiled at her and Susie smiled back with a brief nod. Susie had seen her earlier but hadn't been introduced to her by James, nor had gone anywhere near her. She wondered at the obvious interest in the woman's eyes.

"Tea," the woman said quietly, smiling. "Very English."

"I'm not English, I'm from New Zealand."

"Ah, of course."

The other woman didn't say anything immediately but there was something about her that made Susie approach. "I'm Susie." She extended her hand to the stranger, who accepted her hand in a firm handshake.

"I know."

Susie dropped her hand in confusion as the other woman turned away and blew out some smoke into the night. Then she turned back to her. "I'm Amanda."

Susie frowned briefly. The name meant nothing to her. "Pleased to meet you."

Amanda laughed low and quiet, but without humor. "Pleased? I can see he hasn't told you about me."

A stealthy, sick, chill swept through Susie. She stood quite still. "No, he hasn't."

Amanda's eyes narrowed as she took another drag on her cigarette, openly assessing Susie. "I must say"—she stubbed out the cigarette on the ashtray—"you're not at all how I imagined." While the words could have been offensive, they weren't when combined with the smile, as sweet as spring.

She stepped away from the window, walked up to Susie and picked up a lone glass of champagne. Close up, the woman was even more beautiful—sparkling green eyes, immaculate make-up, and perfect cupid lips colored in the softest shade of pink. But what struck Susie most was the sweet expression on her face. Her perfect lips were twisted in a regretful smile and her eyes had a warmth and sadness that seemed at odds with the rest of her.

"And how exactly did you imagine me?"

"I've been a friend of James for a long time—not his lover *all* that time, you understand, ironic really, considering —and I've seen them come and go, the women I mean. He has great taste."

"Ah, so you see me as an exception to that taste."

"Not at all. You're lovely. Just... different. It must be, as he says. It must be for real this time."

Despite the woman's warm demeanor, despite her smile, Susie was becoming increasingly tense and confused. "I'm sorry, you seem to have the advantage over me. Who are you and what are you to do with James?"

Amanda laughed. "James said you were different and you are. Direct. I like that." She nodded thoughtfully. "I'm pretty sure James was going to ask me to marry him before you appeared on the scene."

The dread and doubt that Susie had kept at bay these last few days rose in a wave, clearing her mind, devastating her heart. Susie opened her mouth to speak but nothing came out. She cleared her throat, looking around, as if for something that would make sense of the woman's words. She turned back to Amanda who was watching her quietly. "Marry?" she whispered.

Amanda nodded. "When James came to see me this afternoon, I knew something had happened. I could see it in his eyes. He'd changed. I was happy for him. Less happy for me, of course. I'm very fond of him and James would have made a superb husband. He didn't love me of course." She shrugged her elegant shoulders. "But that didn't matter. I'd hoped, in time..."

"Didn't matter?" Susie repeated, the words somehow emerging from between numb lips.

"No, because we both would have got what we wanted. As you no doubt know, James loves kids—you have a son I hear?"

Susie nodded.

"And because he can't have any of his own—"

"He can't?" Susie turned away as the pain struck her. James couldn't have kids? Why the hell hadn't he told her? Why did this stranger know more about James than she did? The answer was obvious—because Susie didn't know him at all, because she'd been fooled by him into believing an illusion. The only truth was, Susie had a son and James apparently wanted a family.

Amanda ignored, if she'd ever heard, the question. "And my three kids really needed a father figure. It's hard making ends meet with three children and a bankrupt ex."

Susie shook her head, trying to make sense of the words that seemed to make no sense. "I'm sorry, this is all new to me. You say you thought you were to marry James and that you need money but that it's all now off?" She shook her head. "You must have thought wrong. James, he..." She couldn't continue.

"Not wrong, Susie. We'd talked about it. He wanted to make changes and he'd made it clear I'd be part of them. I'm sorry... I thought you knew. I assumed James had told you, that's why he brought you here."

"No," Susie said. "I wanted to come." She closed her eyes as she remembered how she had insisted. "I wanted to come. I wanted to see where he lived, what his life was like. I hadn't imagined it would be quite this..."

"Illuminating?" Amanda looked awkward. "Look, I'm really sorry. I wouldn't have butted in if I'd thought for one minute you didn't know about us, and our arrangement. It really was more of a business arrangement than anything. Two disillusioned people trying to keep their lives afloat."

For the first time, Susie understood the sadness in this woman's eyes. "I'm sorry."

"That's okay. I've survived worse. I have other options." She gazed around at the open doors to the wine cellar that was full of men, oozing glamour, money and sophistication. "And James has been more than generous with the trust funds. My kids won't want for anything."

"How old are they? Does he know them well? Will he miss them?"

"They'll miss him to begin with but they're too small to remember. Hopefully he'll still get to see them from time to time?"

The sentence ended in a question mark, which Susie knew was down to her to answer. She nodded. "Of course. Whatever James wants. He's a free agent."

"Really? I thought you two were going to get hitched?"

"Look, I'm going now." Susie was unable to think of a

thing further to say to the woman who'd just shattered her vision of the future.

"Sure. Lovely to meet you, Susie, and take good care of James. It looks as if he's found his soul mate after all." Amanda held up her glass in silent salute, finished off the champagne and wandered unsteadily off.

Susie didn't know where she was going but followed Amanda at a distance, back towards the cellar room where the party continued. She watched as Amanda sashayed her way through the crowded room, male eyes turning to watch her walk by. She wanted to hate her but she couldn't. She and James had made a loveless deal because they were desperate, despite the glamour.

She walked up to James and let her hand smooth down the soft, sleek fabric of his expensive tuxedo. "James, we need to talk."

James stopped talking mid-sentence and turned to her, his hand caressing her bare arm. "I'll be with you as soon as I can. Just a few minutes." He tried to slip his arm around her but one of the other men grabbed him, drunkenly reminiscing. James laughed. "You go on up, I'll not be far behind. But I don't know there's much to talk about."

She didn't acknowledge his suggestive words, didn't move her head, her face or her eyes, just looked at him as if he were a stranger, as if she were looking at him from a distance. "We need to talk," she repeated.

She looked around at the group of men who he was chatting to, people she recognized from the wine industry. They took no notice of her, as she expected. She was insignificant, unnoticeable in this glamorous world, wanted only because she could bring James a child, wanted only because she could take James's painful past away because she'd forgiven him, because she trusted him. What a joke!

She stepped away and hesitated but James's attention was soon bound up in the animated conversation with the others. She took another step away and the swirling crowds immediately separated her from James. She knew then that she had to leave.

She'd been wrong and James had been right. There *was* nothing to talk about.

She turned and walked out of the cellar, through the brilliantly lit interiors of the space that now suddenly seemed empty and vast, rather than imposing and brilliant. She walked to the suite she was sharing with James and began to pack.

CHAPTER ELEVEN

Within thirty minutes she was in a taxi, heading back to San Francisco airport with a maxed out credit card and a return flight home booked. She was so lost in her thoughts that it was only when she was offered refreshments that she looked around and realized she'd been ushered into the First-Class Lounge. Then she saw James approaching and she realized why.

He walked over to a room and opened the door. "Susie, you can't go like this. I need to talk to you."

"What the hell is there to say?"

"Give me five minutes. Please."

She followed him into the room and sat down, clutching her bag in front of her, as if it held all the grief in the world and she was determined not to let it spill over. She tried to speak but nothing came out. She cleared her throat. "Five minutes. You have five."

James stayed where he was, leaning against the door, jacketless on this cold night. "Susie, I wanted to tell you—"

"That you were engaged to another woman while you

made love to me? While you insisted I trust you, forgive you? Yes, I can see why you didn't tell me."

"It wasn't like that. You met Amanda. She's a friend, it was an arrangement we thought would suit. It's over. It's all over. I'm so sorry but I never imagined that we could begin again."

"Why didn't you tell me, truly, James, why?"

"Because I was scared you wouldn't understand. I couldn't risk it."

"So you lied to me instead."

She watched him slump back against the door for a moment—his shirt was wet with rain, his tie pulled loose, his eyes hot and intense. "Susie, I—"

She held up her arm to stop him but he came over to her and tried to pull her into his arms. Her stomach plummeted and a dry retch racked her body. She clamped her hand to her mouth and pushed him away, as a cold sweat swept over her. His hand slid down her arm as she tried to escape but he continued to hold her hand in a tight grip, stopping her from leaving his side.

"James, let me go."

"No." He tugged her to him and pulled down her other hand to secure her more firmly to him. "No, not until you listen to me." She looked up into his eyes and for the first time couldn't keep the distance that she'd trained herself to keep. Her eyes filled with tears and she felt them slide down her face, exposing her heart and soul.

"Are you happy now?" she half-choked. "Got what you wanted, James?"

He shook his head and she could see the pain in his eyes. "I wanted to make things better for you, not worse. And they still can be, if you just listen to me."

"I don't *want* to listen to you. Every time I listen to you I

end up believing you, trusting you." She shoved the tears off
her face with the heel of her hand, determined to look him in
the eye with strength. "Do you know what it's like when
you've totally exposed yourself to someone, *given* of yourself,
only to be tossed aside? Only to discover that"—she gulped
in air as she struggled to get the words out—"you *weren't* the
main attraction, you were just some side-dish before the
main show started." She exhaled jerkily. "Go, James. Go off
to your big world with your stupid big ideas and big attrac-
tions. I'm just *me*. Small. Insignificant. Me." She tried to
shake off his hands. "I have to get out of here." She tried to
step towards the door but he still held her hand firmly.

"The flight isn't for another two hours."

"Right." She shook her head, needing the throbbing to
subside so she could think clearly. "I have nowhere to go.
I'm stuck here with you until you decide I can leave."

"You can leave whenever you like."

"Then move out the way."

He gritted his teeth. "Don't do this to me. Don't leave
like this. Not until you've heard me out."

"Why not? Do you think I'm going to embarrass you? Is
that it? I'll embarrass you by telling everyone that I've just
humiliated myself with the one person in the world I
needed to protect myself from? Hey? Don't worry about
that. I'm not leaving. *You* are. Go back to Amanda and that
grand world of yours. It's not my world, never has and never
will be. It's yours. Go."

"I'm not going until you hear me out."

"For pity's sake, James, why won't you just leave?" She
was suddenly aware that she was shivering. Shock, she
thought absently. Shock, because she'd let the worst thing
happen and hadn't even seen it coming until it was too late.

"Not this time. Just listen to me." James brought the sleeve of his silk shirt up and gently wiped away the mascara that had ran down her face. But it made no difference because the tears kept falling. He put his arm around her and brought her to the edge of the sofa and sat her down.

He went to sit beside her. "No!" She shifted away from him and he jumped up as if burned.

He sat down in the chair next to her and pushed his hands through his hair. Behind him the window framed the bright lights of the runway. "I never meant it to be like this. I didn't even imagine we could *ever* be like this again. I had my life and..."

"And you were bored and wanted some amusement. Well, you chose the right woman, didn't you? I'm not one of your sophisticated types who knows what to do when a man seduces her. Never have been and never will be. I guess when you seduced Amanda she knew exactly how to handle you."

He'd been holding his head in his hands but looked up at her then, and the grief in his eyes nearly undid her.

"You're absolutely right. Amanda is an old friend."

"Lucky you. You have so many old friends to choose from."

"She's not as old a friend as you."

"How nice for you. A younger version of me."

"She's nothing like you." He felt for her hand and grabbed it. "Just listen, Suse." He cleared his throat and sucked in a deep breath. "Amanda and I had an arrangement. She doesn't love me and I don't love her."

"You'd marry someone you don't love? What the hell kind of man are you?"

His dull gaze held hers. "A man desperate for a life that isn't filled with emptiness."

"And why would you think a loveless marriage would fill your life?"

"Because it's better than nothing. And nothing was all I had."

"So..." She trailed off, trying to understand. "How would a woman you don't love complete your life?"

He hesitated, holding her gaze. "She has three great kids."

"Oh, yes. I forgot. Stupid me." She exhaled all the confusion, dispelled all her hope in that one word. "Kids. You wanted kids. You can't have them. *Apparently*." She lifted her face slowly to his, the lights of the runway illuminating the smooth planes of his face, enhancing his perfection even further. "So she told me. What was that all about?"

"I... I arranged a vasectomy, soon after I left New Zealand. I was upset over what happened with you. I guess it was some kind of way to punish myself."

"No kids. And you changed your mind and that's why you wanted me. You thought my son, was your son. Your last chance."

"I knew he wasn't mine before we made love. You know it's *you* I want."

"Doesn't sound as if you're too picky about which woman you have, providing she can bring you children." The shakiness, the nausea, the chills had faded away, leaving Susie feeling exhausted but composed. She stood up, opened the door and stood to one side. James didn't move. "Just go."

"I can't leave you like this."

"You have no choice."

"What can I say to show you how much I care for you?"

"Nothing."

He rubbed his hand back and forth against his mouth. "Okay." He dropped his hand, looked out the window and shook his head, opening his mouth to speak but uttering nothing more than gasps of air as the words seemed to evaporate on his lips. He looked at her then and she had to stop herself from walking over to him. He'd always had expressive eyes and the torment and despair in them was plain to see. It reached out to her and touched her, twisting the knife in the raw wound of her heart. His pain was her pain and would always be. She knew that now. She loved him but the truth was she couldn't trust him to love her with the same passion and commitment. He reached out his hand for her. "Susie, please don't go." His voice was bleak with despair and yearning.

She looked at him briefly before stepping towards the door. "James. I have to. Don't you see? If I stay with you now, I'm done. I've given up on myself... and my son. I've more respect for myself than to give myself to someone who professes love for someone while preparing to marry another."

"It was a *business* arrangement, Susie. *Business*. Amanda had suggested it. She'd been through a tricky divorce, she needed money, we got on well. We had a relationship years ago but this wasn't about sex. It was about a future in which we both got what we wanted. She got financial security and I got a home I could return to at night that had children in it, life in it. That's all it was."

"Life is so easy for you, isn't it?"

"If it was, Susie, I wouldn't have to make deals like that one. It's all been second-best since you. I've been running around trying to find what I'd lost when you left my life. But it wasn't to be found. Until I found *you* again. And you slotted into my soul like a missing piece of the puzzle."

"Then why didn't you come to me sooner, James? Why? Okay, I changed my name. But even so, if you'd really wanted to find me you could have done."

"Your last words to me were that you never wanted to see me again. I'd spent a year at Glencoe waiting for you, hoping you'd return. After that I knew you weren't coming back and I didn't try to find out where you were because I didn't think I had any right to know. So I let it go. I let *you* go and waited for the pain to subside. And it did. I kept busy. I held it at bay. But you know what?" He walked over to her and with both hands stroked her hair, his thumbs sweeping her cheeks. "It never went away. I thought I could live with it and then I discovered where you were. And I thought to myself, one last chance before I change my life forever. One last chance for me to help you and in so doing, lessen the knot of pain, shame and love that I held tight inside me. Do us both a favor." He smiled sadly. "I should have known better."

She lifted her hands to his, which now cupped her cheeks. "James, oh James." She closed her eyes against the tears that ran down her face. She gasped in a breath. "How could you have messed this up? How could you?"

He shrugged, trying to dredge some lightness up from deep inside. It didn't work. "It's only important things I mess up. And you're important to me. That knot inside, I'd got so used to it that I had no idea that seeing you would unravel it... would unravel me. It turns out that that knot held a secret, something simple, something very straightfor-ward. My love for you. I love you, Susie. I love you like no one else, I love you with all of my heart and my soul and my body. And... I don't know what else I can say to convince you."

His words swept through her with the warmth of a healing balm, soothing her fears, stimulating her body, but not quieting the nagging voice of distrust in her head. Instinctively she brought her face closer to his. "Words," she whispered against his mouth. He frowned. "Just words, James," she repeated more strongly now. She shifted the palms of her hands over the back of his hands and closed her eyes as she tried to press their shape, size and texture into her mind for a time when she wouldn't have them. Then she gripped them and pulled them from her face. "You're so good with words, they slip off your tongue. I hear your words but I can't *feel* them any more, I can't trust them any more."

"What can I say to make you trust me again?"

"Nothing. No more words. You have to go, now." She counted the seconds against the thumping beat of her heart.

He looked up suddenly and nodded. "No more words. Okay." He didn't move for five of the beats of her heart. "I'll find a way to get through to you, Susie. To make you trust me again. I *have* to because I can't go back to what I was before. It's too late for that."

"Too late," she whispered, whether echoing his words or restating her own thoughts, neither knew for sure. "Just go."

"For now, yes. But I'll be back, Suse."

"Please no. I can't take it. Don't come back to the island with me, James. If you have any small feeling for me, just leave me alone."

"I'll leave, but I'll be back. I can't let you go. I'm sorry, Susie. I'm so sorry." He turned and walked out the door without a backwards glance.

She pressed the door closed and slumped against it, her

whole body trembling. She splayed the palms of her hands against the door, as if she were feeling him, clinging to him, even as she heard his footsteps disappear into the executive lounge.

The return journey to New Zealand slipped by in a blur of strangely dreamless sleep and a dull, dreamlike wakefulness. It was only when Susie first caught sight of the island's wharf from the bow of the ferry that she felt the numbness begin to wear off. She tried to distract herself with a newspaper but, after re-reading the same sentence for ten minutes, she gave up and sat back, closed her eyes and gave herself up to her memories of James.

He filled her mind and heart. For a brief moment in time she'd thought they had a future together, a future free of the mundane practicality and rigid rules she'd run her life by. James was poetry, he was emotion, he was a force that swept her into a realm where she became someone better, the essence of who she was, and who she should be.

But it was all built on nothing. She couldn't believe in that version of herself when it was created on empty words, lying words, words that gave, and at the same time, took away.

She opened her eyes and focused on the people around her. She had to concentrate, she couldn't think of him or else she'd break down and she couldn't break down here. Not yet. She gripped her bag tightly, and sat up taller on the hard seat outside on the deck. People walked by, some she recognized and exchanged rote greetings with. What a difference a few days could make. When she'd left the island she'd been a confident, strong woman who'd been resisting the charms of her ex lover, but the resistance hadn't lasted and she'd fallen into a mire that she couldn't see her way out of.

She disembarked the ferry and caught a taxi up to the winery. It was all so familiar to her and much loved, but now she closed her eyes against it because all she could see was an emptiness where none had been before. She arrived at the winery, paid the taxi and watched it drive away. She didn't know how long she stood looking up at its familiar adobe facade. She practically lived there but now she couldn't face it.

Wearily, she turned and walked down to her house. Tom wasn't due back for days. And nor, officially, was she. She got undressed, pulled on her father's old chenille dressing gown and thick marl socks and curled up on the wicker chair facing the ocean, finally giving way to her feelings, with only the sea as witness.

CHAPTER TWELVE

Forty-eight hours later

James slammed the door of the hire car and looked up at Whisper Creek winery, and around the vineyards, golden in the evening sunlight. His sunglasses protected him from the full blast of the New Zealand sun but, even so, he winced under the glare. He was exhausted. He'd hardly slept in two days, so intent was he on putting to rights the wreckage of his life, on sorting out his business so he could focus on the one thing he knew he wanted.

He glanced at the cottage and locked the car. She'd be at work at this hour. He'd go and find her shortly, just to let her know he was here, if she didn't know already. Only that. Then he'd be gone because he had other plans.

Susie frowned at the sudden knocking that had woken her up. She pulled the dressing gown around her more tightly and made a vague attempt to smooth down her mussed hair. She hadn't left the cottage in two days and she had only one more day before Tom arrived. It couldn't be Tom, though. It was too early. She glanced at the clock—not *that* early maybe. What if something was wrong?

She hurried down the wooden hallway, the yellow walls glowing from the sunlight that poured through the stained glass above the front door. She pulled it open and squinted up into the light. The air pushed out of her lungs and she gripped the handle for support. "James!" She couldn't see his face clearly as the sun was bright behind him but she could sense the tension.

"You haven't been at work."

"You've come here to tell me to get to work?"

"I was worried. You haven't left the cottage in two days. Jorja told me."

She shrugged. "I..."

"Are you okay?"

"I'm...fine." She smoothed down the chunky folds of the dressing gown, but it made no difference. She felt a mess and knew she looked a mess. She drew her arms around herself. "Although I don't see what that has to do with you."

He smiled then. "Still angry then. That's something. I thought you might be sick."

"Is that why you're here? Because you somehow heard I might be sick?"

"Partly. If I could come in I'll explain."

She didn't move but she obviously didn't have as tight a hold on the door handle as she'd imagined because his gentle push opened the door, releasing it from her hands.

"Do I have a choice?"

"Of course. You always have a choice." He didn't move. "Is Tom here?"

"Jorja didn't tell you that?" She sighed. This wasn't the time for sarcasm. "He's due back tomorrow."

James nodded, his brow furrowed. "Right. Look, Susie, I'm sorry I didn't let you know I'd be coming. But I'm not staying, I just wanted to tell you before you heard it from someone else."

Susie's heart dropped. He must mean he was going ahead with the marriage. What else? The sooner he came in, said what he had to say, the better. "Sure." She stepped aside, pulled the belt of the bulky dressing gown more tightly around her and watched as he walked up the hall to the sitting room, ahead of her.

He went straight to the open windows where the white curtains blew in the sea breeze. His shoulders rose and fell as he inhaled deeply. She stopped just behind him. He scanned the deep blue line of the horizon that nestled between the two rocky promontories of the bay. The wind was brisk that morning and the blue of the sea was scuffed with white. The sound of the waves crashing onto the beach filled the air.

"I'd forgotten how beautiful it all is."

She cleared her throat. She mustn't let him get to her. "Wild, is what it is."

"Natural."

"It's beautiful in the Napa Valley. California must have plenty of places more beautiful than this."

He shook his head but didn't speak. When he turned around she saw for the first time the dark shadows under his eyes. She frowned. She'd never seen him look so tired. She fought back an urge to touch him, clenching and unclenching her hands.

"When are you returning?"

He frowned as his eyes searched her face as if looking for clues. But he didn't speak.

"James?"

The spell was suddenly broken and he raised his eyebrows in query. "I'm sorry, Susie. When am I returning?" He shrugged. "I'm not. I've sorted things out with Amanda, as you know. And my business. I'm not returning."

An overwhelming sense of relief filled her but she couldn't let it affect her. So he might not be marrying Amanda but, rightly or wrongly because of her past, she still felt betrayed. "And you've come here to see if I've changed my mind? Because I won't. I told you in California that I don't feel I can trust you. There's nothing you can say that will change my mind."

"I know."

"Then why are you here?"

"I'm moving here, permanently."

She shook her head. "No. I meant it James. You can't just come back and expect me to fall into your arms."

For the first time since his arrival, something like the old smile broke through his serious expression. "Expect? Maybe not. But I can hope."

"Forget it."

"Anyway, that's not what I'm here for now. I'm here to tell you I'm staying at The Lodge for the next few months."

"Why? What?" She couldn't go on. She couldn't form a single rational question from the many that piled up in her brain.

"I made a mistake when I left you once before. I won't be doing that again. I'm not going anywhere this time."

"You're kidding me? Are you going to stalk me or something?"

"Now, there's an idea. But seriously? No, I'm not."

"But, James, what the hell are you going to do with yourself? You're not working at the winery, are you?"

He laughed. "No, of course not. I won't have the time."

Her frown deepened. "Look, am I missing something here? You've cut off your ties from your US business interests, you've moved here, you're not going to be working at the winery and you're not going to be stalking me."

"Correct." He stepped towards her then, his smile gentle as his eyes roved over her obviously confused face. He began to reach up but stopped himself and stepped back. "No stalking, no words of seduction. I'm going to *show* you, Susie, that you can trust me, that I've changed. *Show* you." He didn't wait for her to reply. But gave a tight, rueful smile, looked down at his dusty shoes and walked away down the hallway.

Dumbfounded, Susie didn't move, simply watched him open the door to the bright sunlight, its beams spotlighting her for a brief moment before the door was closed. James was gone, and the cottage felt emptier than ever.

For the fourth day running, Susie stepped out onto the deck into the bright morning sunshine and watched as James untied the small motor boat from the jetty at the other end of the bay. He was dressed in casual jeans and t-shirt, carrying a box of something heavy by the looks of things. He dropped it into the boat followed by a rucksack that he'd had on his back. A rucksack? Since when did James Mackenzie own, let alone carry, a rucksack? Not since he was twelve years old, she suspected.

She narrowed her gaze as she tried to piece together the clues. She had no idea where he was going, what he was doing, or anything about how he'd been spending his time over the past few days. Like before, he didn't turn to look at her although the bay was small and he must surely have been aware of her. But there was no acknowledgement.

Susie fidgeted as the realization struck her that she wanted him to notice her. She banged her booted foot against the post, ostensibly trying to shift the dried mud, but it wasn't the mud that was agitating her. He'd kept his word —he hadn't stalked her, in fact he'd ignored her. The only time she saw him was every morning and evening, getting into a boat and getting out of a boat. Her only communication had been by email in reply to any business matter she needed him to know about. Otherwise, there had been silence. He'd always left The Lodge by the time she arrived at the winery in the morning, not arriving back to the bay until late in the evening.

What was he up to? She hadn't a clue because she hadn't asked and no one was telling her.

And she didn't want to know. Of course she didn't. He'd simply come up with some weird and wonderful scheme to get her interested. He'd grow bored. He'd soon be gone because that was what James did, didn't he?

She locked the cottage and walked up to the winery. As soon as she entered the wine-tasting room, the women fell quiet.

"Don't mind me," she muttered, as she walked through to the winery.

She heard the murmurs begin again before she'd shut the door, like waves closing in behind her. She shook her head. The sooner he went the better. Then why did she feel so different? The buzz of excitement she'd felt at seeing him again had refused to leave her, despite her best arguments. If he could seduce her while preparing to propose to someone else, what else could he do?

She sighed and tried to focus on her work. She grunted

and backspaced her reply to James's email. She picked up her cell phone and hit the text button. She'd find out. She had a right to know.

Where are you? Need some papers signed.

It was a lie but she'd think of something. The reply came almost immediately.

Will sign tonight.

She bit her lip and tapped her phone on the table. Okay, so he was being cagey. What the hell was he hiding? She jumped up and walked around the winery until she found Jorja.

"Time for a coffee?"

Jorja raised her eyebrows in surprise. "Coffee? Sure, why not." She dropped her clipboard onto the desk and followed Susie out to the cafe. She sat back, put her feet up on the rough table and crossed her arms.

Susie felt distinctly uncomfortable. She smiled slightly and then turned away, trying to work out how to broach the subject. "Work going okay?"

"You know it is." Jorja's lips twitched with amusement but she didn't say anything further. There was a silence as the waiter brought them two steaming mugs of coffee. "The new machinery Guy recommended is due in next week and we're all set to receive it. The grapes are looking good on the vine. But you know all that. Anything else you need to know?"

"I just wondered..." How the hell was she going to ask Jorja whether she knew what James was up to?

Jorja tilted her head to one side, the grin broadening. "Yes?"

Susie sighed and sat back. "You know what I'm wondering."

Jorja shrugged. "Don't know for sure until you ask."

"I just wondered..." Susie swallowed as she tried to work out the best way of wording her query. She really didn't want everyone to know that she and James hadn't spoken to each other over the past few days and yet she really needed to know what he was doing. "You know"—she poked the sugar bowl with a spoon—"whether you think James will be finished any time soon." She bit her lip. "Finished with... what he's doing," she added, wincing at her attempt at subterfuge.

"Doubt it. It's a big job." To Susie's irritation, Jorja didn't elaborate but continued to sip her coffee.

"Yes, I guess it is." Susie sighed.

"Got any idea about what it's going to be?"

Susie narrowed her gaze onto her coffee, trying to work out the best answer. "No." Short but to the point.

"Us neither. There's been all sorts of rumors about what's going to happen to it, but James won't answer my questions directly and no one else has dared ask him."

"Um." Susie's mind raced as she tried to work out what the "it" was that was causing the gossip. Then she stopped, the coffee mug raised half-way to her mouth, as it suddenly hit her. The boat could take him anywhere—to Auckland, to other parts of the island, to other islands in the Gulf—but why always the boat? She returned the mug to the table. Because there was no road access. "So..." She looked up at Jorja and smiled, for the first time comfortable that she was on the right track. "Pete's old homestead. What's been happening with it?" She tried to control the thudding in her heart as she remembered their time together at the bay.

Jorja shrugged. "Don't know. Haven't been there."

"Perhaps Pete has plans for the place? I wonder why he hasn't told us."

"Well, for one thing he's living in the middle of

nowhere, and for another, he's in love." Jorja leaned forward. "Know what that's like?"

Susie didn't meet Jorja's narrowed gaze, but continued to concentrate with unusual interest on her coffee. "So perhaps James is working with Pete to finish off what nature has started."

"Demolish it, you mean?" Jorja shook her head. "No."

"Really? How can you be so certain?"

"Because...what would be the point of having tonnes of new wood delivered to the bay if the house is to be pulled down."

Susie sat forward, forgetting her attempt to be casual. "What? Tell me everything you know."

"Ha! I wondered how long it would take. I saw Mike, my brother-in-law, down the pub. You remember Mike? Tall, big guy, beard. Really bad beard, actually, it's—"

"Jorja!"

"Well, he told me that his sister's fiance works for the big builder's merchant in Auckland and they've been delivering building supplies direct to the bay for a week."

"He's having it rebuilt." Susie muttered the words in wonderment to herself.

"Oh no, he's not."

"He's not? But what about the building materials?"

"Susie. He's not got anyone working for him."

"So what the hell is James doing there?"

Jorja pursed her lips and raised both eyebrows. "I can only guess. But I reckon it's about time you came out from that closed world you've been living in ever since your return from the States, opened your eyes and looked around you. *You* find out what he's up to."

"What do you mean?"

"Exactly, Susie, as I say."

"You're calling me Susie, now, not Susannah."

"Yep, guess I am. James is right, it suits you. He sees you for who you are, Susie. He loves you for who you are. Why can't you see that?"

"The question isn't whether I can see it or not. It's whether I accept it."

Jorja dropped her legs back to the ground and leaned towards Susie. "Give me one good reason why not?"

"Because." Susie sprang up and away from Jorja and folded her arms as she paced across the small courtyard. "Because, Jorja, I'm scared. You don't know him. He does what he likes, when he likes, to whom he likes. And then"— she swallowed as she tried to keep her emotions inside— "and then he... leaves."

"And you're waiting for that moment are you?"

"I can't trust him. I just can't. I've got too much to lose. What if Tom grew to love him and then James left. And what if I..." She couldn't bring herself to finish the sentence.

"Too late for that I think. Susie, I've *seen* you with James. I've seen the way he looks at you and I've seen how you respond to him." She sat back, sighing. "You're the most damn natural couple I've ever seen together. And I've seen a lot."

Susie fiddled with her fingers as she looked away out to the grapevines and the ridge. "But there's more to life than liking someone, than wanting to be with someone. There's security, there's reliability, there's knowing that something, or someone, is there for you. There's trust." She turned to Jorja. "I don't trust him. I can't trust him. I have to protect me and Tom."

"From what? Happiness? A loving family? I'd risk it like a shot. James is gorgeous and he's clearly head over heels in love with you."

"He hasn't talked to me in days."

"Oh, yeah, you're right. He's probably gone off you big time. It's probably nothing to do with the fact you no doubt told him to leave you alone."

"Well... I guess."

Jorja sighed. "Susie. Stop guessing and just go and find out what he's doing. It's not a commitment, it's just a step. Take it." She finished her coffee and bounced up. "I've got to go. I've work to do. I've got to cover two jobs this afternoon. *Yours*... and mine." She grinned at Susie and returned inside, leaving Susie unsure about her feelings, unsure about her future, but certain of only one thing. She needed to know what James was doing.

Susie dragged the dinghy off the sands and into the sea. Once it was beyond the small breakers she switched on the motor and she was soon out of her bay and around the headland. The day was glorious, a warm breeze and only tufts of white clouds scooting high overhead. The cold sea splashed over her warm skin as she bounced across the current and followed the coastline around to the more remote part of the island where the land was still covered in bush and cut off by plunging gullies. She slowed as she rounded the headland into the bay. As the beach came into sight she sat back as if pushed and just stared.

Where once there'd been an unbroken line of bush and pohutukawa trees, now the old homestead stood, clearly visible from the square widow's walk at the top, down to the full-length verandahs that ran across the front on both the first and ground floor. All of it covered with scaffolding. To one side the stream emerged and ran down to the beach, fanning into tributaries on the low tide. Red-billed sand-pipers delicately picked their way over the sands.

She cut the engine and drifted up to the jetty, throwing a loop of rope around the end. She pulled the boat around and climbed up the steps.

There was no sound other than the birds and throbbing cicadas in the bush and the breaking of the lively waves on the shore. His boat was here but there was no sign of James. Then suddenly she heard him. The regular back and forth of a saw on wood, coming from inside the house.

She could hardly believe it had only been a few short weeks since she'd been there with Tom... with James. She'd been aware of a sense of completeness then and she felt it again now as she listened to the rhythmic sawing. She smiled as she remembered how he'd loved to work on the tree house, on fences, on anything with his hands, much to the consternation of his mother, who had no intention of allowing any of her sons to become carpenters.

Piles of equipment and timber had been dragged up to the beach and stored in orderly stacks under tarpaulin. Scaffolding had been erected around the house on all sides. She stopped in front of the wide sweep of steps that led to the front door. She'd always entered by the back door, as they'd done before because the front had been covered with creepers and trees. Now she could see just how beautiful a home it was... and could be.

She was suddenly aware of a silence. The sawing had stopped. She walked up to the steps and onto the verandah, her gaze sweeping to the ceiling, which was in the process of being repaired.

"Don't move!" Shocked, she turned around. James was carefully picking his way towards her.

"Why not?"

"Because." He reached her and took her hand in both of his, caressing it tenderly. "I haven't finished working on this yet. There are still some rotten boards need sorting out." He smiled. "Place your feet where I put mine and watch where you're going." Susie looked down and saw the rotten and missing floor boards she'd failed to see when she'd been too busy looking up and around. But, more than that, she felt the heat of his hand encasing hers as he led her to safety.

Once off the verandah, he didn't drop her hand, but led her to the back step. There he had a comfortable chair, a small gas stove, chilly bin and other evidence that he might be working on the house, but he certainly wasn't going to be uncomfortable while he did it. "Have a seat. Would you like a drink? Kettle's just boiled."

She couldn't help but laugh. "Sure. A cup of Earl Grey tea please. Any lemon?"

"Can do the tea, but no lemon, I'm afraid."

"Your standards are slipping."

"I wasn't expecting the pleasure of your company. Not yet anyway."

There was silence and they just looked at each other. She felt her resolve begin to disintegrate. She breathed in sharply and looked around. "You've bought it from Pete then?"

"Yes. He's sold me the house and a good bit of land around it."

"I had no idea."

"It all happened quickly. Pete was more than happy because he knew what I planned. He'd been fighting off investors for years who wanted to develop the area for housing, farming whatever. This way it reverts to what it was like originally."

She raised her eyebrows in surprise as she accepted the

cup of tea from him and sat down. "Originally? How do you mean? This is for the new lodge, right?"

James shrugged. "Maybe. Maybe not. I'll decide after I've discussed the matter with my executive team."

"Who?"

"You. There's no need to decide immediately. My team of builders won't arrive for a few months yet."

"But you've made a start by yourself?"

"Yes. For now, it's me. I wanted to make a start myself. I *needed* to."

She nodded, unable to take her eyes off him. His usually immaculate hair had traces of sawdust through it and his hands were roughened and scratched. His clothes were splashed with paint and his work boots were new. But the dark circles had all but disappeared and his eyes were less restless, his smile when it settled on her was relaxed and content. "You're having fun here aren't you?"

"Sure am. I used to try to get involved with the company's property developments but there were always other things I needed to do to keep things running, keep the money coming in."

"I guess you don't have to worry about money any more."

"I've more than enough with the business interests I've retained." He looked up at the house, his hand smoothing down some weatherboards that had just been sanded. "I can run them from here."

"You're going to make your home here, then?" She asked cautiously.

He grinned. "You only just got that?"

"I wanted to hear it from you."

"Yes. My home's here all right. I've never felt more sure of anything." He glanced at her. "Or nearly anything."

She knew he meant her and she breathed in deeply as she allowed her remaining defenses to crumble completely. She stood up. "I'm surprised you're not camping here."

"Are you? I might have made a massive lifestyle change but I haven't completely lost my mind."

"Oh, I thought you enjoyed camping with me and Tom."

He walked up behind her and slipped his arms around her shoulders. "You know I did. But that was all about the company, not sleeping on hard ground."

She stilled and closed her eyes at his touch but she didn't move away. She sighed and turned in his arms. "So, you've bought a house, you're doing it up, you think I should trust you now?"

He looked surprised. "No, I've only been here a few days. I don't expect anything from you just because I've committed to a house, to a place... to a woman, forever."

The word "forever" stuck in her mind. Forever was a long time. You could trust someone if they were with you forever. "Good." She slipped her hands up to his chest and smoothed them over the soft fabric of his t-shirt. "Because I can't imagine what 'forever' means."

"You don't have to. You just have to live it. Day by day."

"One step at a time then?" She lifted her face to his and he reached down and kissed her softly on the lips. She sighed and laid her cheek against his chest and breathed him in.

"One step at a time."

EPILOGUE

Six months later...

Susie waved at the departing launch and smiled to see Guy putting his arm protectively around a very pregnant Lucia.

James came up beside her and pulled a cork from a bottle of wine and sniffed it. "It's going to be a good year."

"Not least for Lucia." Susie smiled at the recollection of just how happy Lucia had been.

James followed Susie's gaze at the launch as it passed out of the bay and around the corner, waving at the departing figures. "She deserves it, they both deserve it. But twins? Good luck to them."

"They'll be brilliant. It's a dream come true for them both."

She took the glass of wine from him and looked up at the immaculately restored verandah, its fresh white paint gleaming in the cool winter sunshine. The sound of a tune being picked out on the piano drifted out to them through open windows.

"And what about your dreams, Susie? Have they come true?"

"Are you kidding? Listen to that." They both listened as Tom continued to play the piano, his musicality and sense of enjoyment obvious, despite the simplicity of the piece. The music suddenly stopped and Tom came running out, his eyes bright with excitement.

"I got to the end! Did you hear me?"

"We heard!" they both exclaimed in unison. James ruffled the boy's hair and Tom returned inside.

"He's so happy."

"And are you, Suse? When you sit at the top of the cliff and look out at the sky, what do you dream of?"

"Nothing in particular. It's the feeling I get from sitting there, that I like. With the wind on my face and the birds flying just out of reach, it's as if I'm flying too. Flying free, no restrictions."

"You don't like restrictions, then." He sighed and she turned to him, surprised at his doleful tone. "And there I was about to ask you if you'd have my babies."

She nearly choked on her wine. "James! But—" she spluttered.

"I'd hoped," he continued calmly as if she hadn't just spilt her wine on the newly painted floorboards. "That the last six months had been enough."

"Enough to...?"

"To convince you that, like it or not, I'm never leaving you." He pulled her into his arms and she wriggled against him.

"I like it."

He caressed her face and the look he gave her made her melt. "Yes, I can see that in your eyes."

She wriggled closer into his embrace. "You can read me so easily, hey?"

"Sure."

"What am I thinking now?"

He shrugged and drew in a considered breath. "You're wondering where I went yesterday."

"No, I wasn't. Well, maybe, just a bit. I was waiting for you to tell me."

"And I was waiting until we were alone." He pulled back and watched her carefully. "I went to see the doctor."

"What about?"

"I asked him what the chances were of reversing the operation."

"The vasectomy?"

"Yeah."

"And?"

"He can do the operation all right. But there are no guarantees that it will work."

A slow smile spread over Susie's face. "I thought you'd given up any idea of having children."

"No, you just assumed I had."

"So... do you want children?"

"Put it this way, I think I want to try. A lot."

She slid her arm around his body. "Is that right?" She reached up and kissed him.

"But I won't do it if it's too difficult for you to deal with. I don't want you to get your hopes up for nothing."

"James, whatever happens will be a bonus, it'll be something I never anticipated. I want to be with you, period. I think we should marry."

He swallowed and tried to hide his emotions behind a wry grin. He brushed her hair from her face. "I've been waiting to hear that. You know I'd have proposed on day one but I needed it to come from you."

"I want to be with you, by your side, taking the good and bad."

"Bad? You think I'm going to let anything bad happen to you?"

"No, I don't." Her voice was muffled against his neck. "I trust you."

"Good." He pulled away and they walked down the steps to the beach. "Because I reckon if it works out, we should have a big family."

"A lot of kids? They're hard work, you know."

"I'm up for it. How does seven sound?"

"James! You're crazy. It sounds way too many. What about two?"

"Two? We'd have an odd number then. Tom plus two. No. But we could go with five."

"Five! No way. Three?"

They reached the water's edge and James turned her in his arms and they both looked up at the house, with Tom's music spilling outside onto the beach. They stopped there and James held Susie's face in his hands as if it were the most precious thing on earth.

"I love you, Suse." He pressed his lips to hers briefly before settling a small kiss on the indentation of her top lip. "But..." He pressed another kiss to the corner of her smiling lips. "Five..." Another to the other side. "It..." And one in the bottom curve of her lips. "Is..."

AFTERWORD

Thank you for reading *Second Chance at Whisper Creek*. I hope you enjoyed it! *Second Chance at Whisper Creek* is the fifth book in The Mackenzies series. An excerpt follows of the next book in the series—*Summer at the Lakehouse Café* —which features Pete and Lizzi. The Mackenzies series consists of:

A Place Called Home (Guy and Lucia)
Secrets at Parata Bay (Dallas and Cassandra)
Escape to Shelter Springs (Callum and Gemma)
What you See in the Stars (Morgan and Rebecca)
Second Chance at Whisper Creek (James and Susie)
Summer at the Lakehouse Café (Pete and Lizzi)

Happy reading!

Sophie

SUMMER AT THE LAKEHOUSE CAFÉ
BOOK 6 OF THE MACKENZIES—PETE

A staunchly independent solo mum. A wine-maker who has lost his family. A summer in which to learn to trust again.

Lizzi Burnett part owns and runs The Lakehouse Café. But

*when her abusive ex-husband wants her to sell unless she
can pay him out, she's determined that she'll do it her way or
not at all. Because she refuses to trust anyone with her or her
daughter, Aimee's, lives.*

*She won't even trust Pete, who she first meets emerging from
the lake like a god—or at least like a kiwi Daniel Craig. Pete
has re-located to New Zealand's Mackenzie country to start
afresh. His family are all dead and he wants to move forward
with his life... move forward with Lizzi and Aimee.*

*But what he doesn't realize is that the hurt he sees in Lizzi's
eyes is only a fraction of what lies hidden, deep inside her.
And it'll take a whole lot of soul-searching and loving to heal
that...*

Excerpt

Lizzi sat on the sand, and leaned against the side of an
upturned dinghy, just outside the circle of firelight. Pete sat
beside her.

"Thanks for inviting me, Lizzi. I realize you probably
did it out of selfless pity for someone alone during a holiday
weekend. And I'm afraid I accepted it out of a selfish desire
to hang out with you and your family."

Lizzi paused. Why exactly had she invited him? "No,
really, I thought it would be—"

"It's okay," Pete interrupted. "Whatever impulse made
you extend the invitation, it's all right by me."

He looked straight ahead, over the flames toward where
Max, Amber, Rachel and Gabe sat, laughing at some family
joke.

"I miss that," Pete said.

"What?"

Pete indicated the group the other side of the fire pit with his beer bottle. "That closeness. The familiarity. The short-hand family uses, knowing that the others will understand. It's a solid foundation of love which you take for granted until it's gone."

Pete rested his head against the dinghy, still looking straight ahead, his profile lit by the darting flames, the shadows they created revealing more of his strength than the most brilliant light could have done.

"I'm sorry," she said, wincing at the lameness of her response. She couldn't think of any words that could convey how much she understood and felt his pain. "And thank you for showing me what's in front of me, but which I hardly notice. I get so wrapped up in my own things. Aimee, the café, money..."

He turned to her then. "I don't notice *you* anywhere on that list."

She gave a brief laugh. "I guess I got left off so long ago I can't remember me being there."

"Then maybe you should add yourself. To the top, I reckon."

"I'm a mother," she said softly. "My child will always be at the top of my list."

As if on cue, Aimee left her position within Rachel's arms and stumbled over to Lizzi. "I'm tired, Mum," said Aimee, yawning, as she fell into Lizzi's lap.

Lizzi put her arms around Aimee and pulled her tight against her in a big hug. Aimee nestled into Lizzi's embrace, and Lizzi kissed the top of her head as Aimee yawned. She pulled the shawl from around her shoulders and covered Aimee who snuggled under its warmth. And there, at that moment, Lizzi realized the truth of Amber's words. She *was* lucky. And, she realized the truth of Pete's words. It didn't matter what else happened, she'd always have her family.

"Lizzi, what's up? Are you crying?" whispered Pete, his head close to hers. She pursed her lips and nodded, unable to stop the tears from falling down her cheeks, as both hands still held the now sleeping Aimee.

Pete brought his finger against her cheek and swept the tears away. He put his arm around her, and she leaned against him. None of her siblings seemed to notice anything was different. None of them looked at them askance. There were no raised eyebrows, or grins, to question her earlier assertions that Pete and she were just friends. They simply didn't appear to notice. Maybe they'd all got it right, mused Lizzi, and it was *her* that was slow on the uptake. Because being in the arms of Pete Marshall sure felt right.

ALSO BY SOPHIE HAYDON

The Mackenzies

A Place Called Home

Secrets at Parata Bay

Escape to Shelter Springs

What you See in the Stars

Second Chance at Whisper Creek

Summer at the Lakehouse Café

Lantern Bay

Yours to Give

Yours to Treasure

Yours to Cherish

Yours to Keep

Yours Forever

Yours to Love

ABOUT THE AUTHOR

Hello!

My name is Sophie Haydon and I write romances with stories which make you turn the pages, and characters who feel real.

I'm an avid people watcher, hopeless romantic and dreamer who spends far too much time gazing out the window, imagining scenes where people struggle with life and emotions but always end up happily. Because, yes, I'm also an eternal optimist!

I currently have two connected series — Mackenzies and Lantern Bay — which feature the Mackenzie and Connelly families. At the moment, I'm writing the fifth Lantern Bay book, but am already planning future series.

All the books I've written so far are set in New Zealand, where I live. But I was born on the north Norfolk coast of England and am planning a series set in the small seaside town in which I grew up. And then there's my Nantucket trilogy which I began planning years ago, but have yet to find time to write.

So, wherever you are in the world, welcome to my little corner, where I sit with my two cocker spaniels snoring gently beside me, creating worlds where people struggle with life and emotions but are always rewarded with love and happiness in the end. Because that's non negotiable!

I hope you enjoy my books.

Sophie

x